P9-DNX-571

SPHDZ
Book #3!

Ten Points of Articulation by
Steven Weinberg

headz

by Jon Scieszka

Swivel Action by Casey Scieszka

Illustrated by Shane Prigmore

Simon & Schuster Books for Young Readers
New York London Toronto Sydney New Delhi SPHDZ

SIMON
BO
An
Ch
12
Ne
Th references to historical
people, or sly. Other names, ch aces,
and incidents are products or's imagination, and an
ual events or locales or ersons, living or dead, is entire

FOR ADE
Sim Sch information
out special purchase
t Simon & Special les
50 or ss@ ste
Bureau to
ent or informati to
kers 1-866
rs.co Dan
The te this b Jopp illustrations for
Manufactured in the United States
of Am 811
2 4 6

Libr ess Cataloging-in-Publication
Scieszka, J
SPHDZ boo ! / Jon Scieszka ; illu
trated by Prig
Casey Sciesz points of articulati
by Steven W erg
(Sp eadz ; 3)
only one hun
to cha
ng Earth-saving
s t ainwave
ore ose.
ISBN 1-41 955-5 ver : al per)
[1. Extraterrestr Fic washing—Fiction.
3. Schools—Fictio 4. 5. endship—Fiction.
6. Family life—Ne rk ion. 7. Brooklyn
(New York, N.Y.)—] I. ll. II. Scieszka,
y. en. IV. Title. V. Title: SPHDZ mber three!
7.S [Fic]—dc23 2011029872
SB 1 296-5 (eBook)

To you, you, an

Thanks for joining th ve.

We could not have d .

—J.

To Madison, Mackenzie, and Noah, t ziest S IDZ ses d DZ

nep ola

SIMON & SCHUSTER
BOOKS FOR YOUNG READERS
An imprint of Simon & Schuster
Children's Publishing Division
1230 Avenue of the Americas,
New York, New York 10020

 • For information about special discounts for bulk purchases, please contact Simon & Schuster Special Sales at 1-866-506-1949 or business@simonandschuster.com. •

The Simon & Schuster Speakers Bureau can bring authors to your live event. For more information or to book an event, contact the Simon & Schuster Speakers Bureau at 1-866-248-3049 or visit our website at www.simonspeakers.com. • Book design by Dan Potash • The text for this book is set in Joppa. • The illustrations for this book are rendered digitally. • Manufactured in the United States of America • 0811 FFG

2 4 6 8 10 9 7 5 3 1

Library of Congress Cataloging-in-Publication Data

Scieszka, Jon.

SPHDZ book #3! / by Jon Scieszka ; illustrated by Shane Prigmore ; swivel action by Casey Scieszka ; 10 points of articulation by Steven Weinberg. — 1st ed.

p. cm. — (Spaceheadz ; 3)

Summary: With only one hundred more Spaceheadz to sign up, Michael K.'s friends start planning an Earth-saving party but Michael fears the Brainwave might be used for a much more sinister purpose.

ISBN 978-1-4169-7955-5 (hardcover : alk. paper)

[1. Extraterrestrial beings—Fiction. 2. Brainwashing—Fiction. 3. Schools—Fiction. 4. Spies—Fiction. 5. Friendship—Fiction. 6. Family life—New York (State)—New York—Fiction. 7. Brooklyn (New York, N.Y.)—Fiction.] I. Prigmore, Shane, ill. II. Scieszka, Casey. III. Weinberg, Steven. IV. Title. V. Title: SPHDZ book number three!

PZ7.S41267Sof 2011 [Fic]—dc23 2011029872

ISBN 978-1-4424-1296-5 (eBook)

To you, you, and especially you.

Thanks for joining the Spaceheadz Brainwave.

We could not have done it without you.

—J. S.

To Madison, Mackenzie, and Noah, the craziest SPHDZ nieces and SPHDZ nephew on the planet

—S. P.

DUNK
DUNKER'S
ER'S

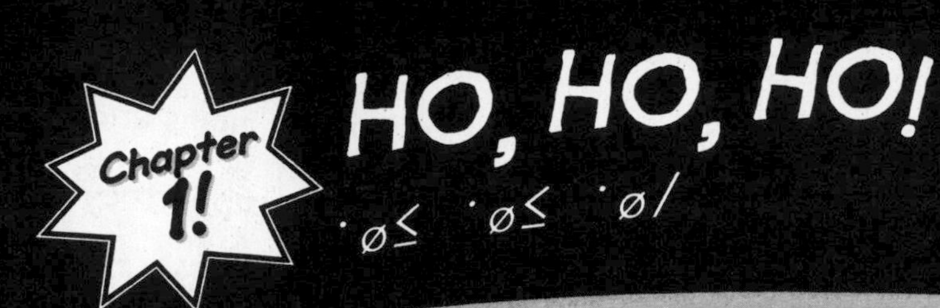

Chapter 1! HO, HO, HO!

Two small elves stood in line behind the red ropes outside Dunker's Donuts on Fifth Avenue in Brooklyn.

This was not as completely crazy as it might sound, because there was also a sign in the Dunker's Donuts window that read:

The two elves stood in line with the rest of the moms and dads and babies and kids waiting to tell Santa what they really wanted. The two elves wore those green elf outfits you've seen in cartoons and movies and cookie commercials.

But the strange thing about these two elves was that one of them wore soccer cleats and the other one wore a SpongeBob SquarePants backpack . . . that was carrying another tiny, hamster-size elf.

"What are you going to ask Santa to bring you, Chelsea?" the mom in front of the elves asked her daughter.

"A pony," said Chelsea, kicking her little brother.

"Oooooh," said the SpongeBob-backpack elf. "More flavor! I'm going to add a pony to our list."

"We are already asking Santa for one hundred more SPHDZ," said soccer-cleats elf. "Can he also fit two ponies in his flying-sled delivery system?"

"Eeek squeak squeak eeek," said hamster elf. "Squeee week wee eek."

"Great whole-grain jingle bells!" said soccer-cleats elf. "This Santa Claus is super-size and great taste!"

"Eee eee eee eeek?" asked hamster elf.

"Yes," said backpack elf. "That is a most extra-crunchy idea. I will send a visual image of us to Michael K. and Venus."

"Ho, ho, ho," said the suspiciously skinny-looking Santa in the Holidayz HoHoHoles Korner of the Dunker's Donuts. "I don't think Santa will be able to get you a real F-18 Hornet fighter jet."

The little boy in Santa's lap punched Santa in his red velvet stomach and pulled Santa's white beard down under his chin. "You are a stupid Santa."

The backpack elf held a camera out at arm's length.

"Squeeek," said the hamster elf.

The elves twisted their faces into something like smiles.

The hamster elf nodded.

The camera took a picture.

"Come on, Jackson," said the little boy's mom. "We will go talk to Santa's manager about this."

The dad took Jackson's hand and glared at Santa. "I can't believe I had to buy a dozen Holidayz HoHoHoles for this. All you had to do was say 'Okay.'"

"I could look into procurement of the F-18," said Santa, replacing his beard and fixing his stomach. "But I am pretty sure it is not in line with federal procedure to release these fighter jets to citizens."

The dad stared at Santa.

"There would also be a lot of paperwork. But maybe the older model F-111 might be available?"

Now both the mom and the dad were staring at Santa.

Santa realized he had almost forgotten to say the required Dunker's Holiday Saying. He added, "Ho, ho, ho. Dunker's knows what dunkers love."

The mom and dad and punching kid stormed over to talk to the manager.

The line and the elves moved three steps closer to Santa.

Hamster elf sent off the picture and text.

"Eeee eee, eee eee."

"**CLINICALLY PROVEN SAFE AND EFFECTIVE**," added backpack elf. "Michael K. and Venus are going to be sooooo surprised!"

Michael K. and Venus sat at the table farthest away from the librarian.

Venus flipped open her sparkly and SPHDZ-stickered laptop and logged on to the library's free wireless.

"Check this out," whispered Venus.

Venus launched spaceheadz.com and quickly clicked

"Spaceheadz drawings from Magic BBQ Sauce in Seattle, Washington . . .

"Spaceheadz ads from Toll-Free Fusilli in Lebanon, Indiana . . .

"Spaceheadz music from All-Natural Oven Cleaner in Toronto, Ontario . . .

"Spaceheadz stories from Bold Taste Deodorant in London, England . . .

"Spaceheadz videos from Disposable Chicken Fingers in Barcelona, Spain . . .

"We really did it, Michael K.," whispered Venus. "We really connected a whole Spaceheadz network."

"Wow," said Michael K.

He had been so busy going to school, spreading the Spaceheadz word, and trying to keep Bob and Jennifer and Major Fluffy out of trouble . . . that he hadn't stopped to look at the whole thing. It was pretty amazing.

"And coolest of all . . . ," whispered Venus. She clicked back to the Spaceheadz home page and zoomed in on the counter. "We are almost at our three point one four million plus one Spaceheadz to save the world."

Michael K. read the Spaceheadz counter aloud, "Three million one hundred thirty-nine thousand nine hundred and one Spaceheadz? WOO!"

The librarian, at the other end of the room, gave Michael K. a stern look.

Michael K. ducked his head.

"This is great. This is huge. I can't believe we are going to do it," whispered Michael K. "Only one hundred more Spaceheadz to go. This is amazing."

Michael K. stared at the spaceheadz.com counter. Then he had another thought.

"But what if something goes wrong?"

Venus clicked through more Spaceheadz drawings and Spaceheadz ads. "You are such a downer sometimes. We haven't seen the AAA in weeks. And Bob, Jennifer, and Major Fluffy have been almost normal. What could go wrong?"

"I don't know," said Michael K. "You know how weird stuff just seems to happen with Spaceheadz."

Venus ignored Michael K. She clicked happily through more Spaceheadz pages. "'SPHDZ **DOES IT BETTER!**'

'I'M A SPHDZ / YOU'RE A SPHDZ / WOULDN'T YOU LIKE TO BE A SPHDZ TOO?' 'MAKE FRIENDS WITH SPHDZ, MAKE SPHDZ WITH FRIENDS!' Spaceheadz kids are geniuses!

"And check this out," said Venus. "Our three point one four million plus one moment is going to be historic. I'm recording the final counter moments in the Spaceheadz admin section so we can have them forever."

Venus clicked on the tiny words SPHDZ ADMIN at the bottom right corner of the spaceheadz.com page, right next to TERMS OF USE and PRIVACY POLICY. It opened a page asking for another password. Venus typed VENUS. The secret recording page popped onscreen. "Cool, huh?"

"Yeah," said Michael K., trying to ignore the feeling in his gut. "That is cool. What could go wrong?"

Michael K.'s phone and Venus's phone buzzed with incoming texts at exactly the same time.

Michael K. checked the sender.

MAJOR FLUFFY

Michael K. opened the message. It read:

EEEEK EEE EEE EEEE EEEK.

Michael used "Fluffy's Translator" to translate the message into English.

MORE FLAVOR! DELICIOUS IDEA.
ASKING NOW OF SANTA FOR MORE SPHDZ!

This message made Michael K. a bit nervous. Michael K. looked at the picture.

This made him completely freaked out.

"AHHHHHGGGG!" croaked Michael K., pointing at the picture.

"WHAT?" said Venus.

"EEE ARRR GAHHH UHHH!"

Michael K. was so spazzed out that he could not manage to say any real words. He pointed at the face over elf Bob's shoulder.

"That's cute," said Venus. "The Spaceheadz are visiting Santa."

Michael K. zoomed in on the face revealed by the pulled-down Santa beard.

Michael K. regained just enough power of speech to yell four words.

"Not Santa! Agent Umber!"

The librarian got up from her desk to remove the noisemakers from the quiet room.

But Michael K. and Venus were already out the door, running like the future of the world depended on it.

And it did.

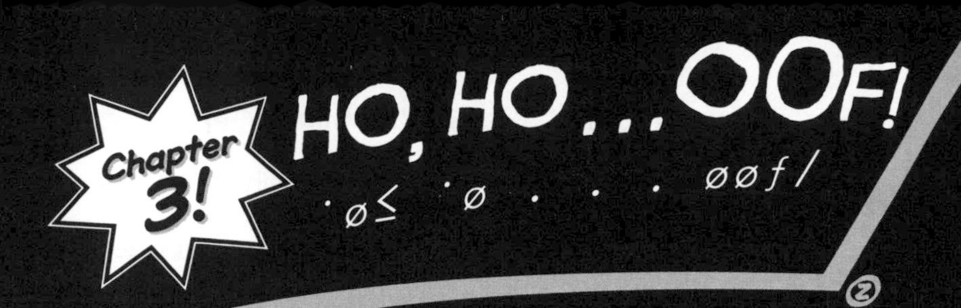

"I can't believe I had to buy a dozen Holidayz HoHoHoles for this. All you had to do was say 'Okay,'" said the man in front of Agent Umber.

Agent Umber pulled his Santa beard back up and readjusted his padded Santa stomach.

Santa wanted to be a good Santa. He really did. And he really did not want to get in any more trouble with his Dunker's boss. Because trouble with his Dunker's boss would only mean trouble with the chief. And Umber did not want more trouble.

This deep cover as Santa, in a doughnut shop, already combined two of Umber's worst nightmares. (See the AAA's Fried Santa Incident and Agent Sienna File.) He didn't need to add any more.

So Santa Umber explained just a little bit about federal fighter-jet policy. Then he remembered to say the required Dunker's Holiday Saying: "Ho, ho, ho. Dunker's knows what dunkers love."

Another kid climbed up into Santa Umber's lap.

"***HO, HO, HO,***" said Santa Umber. "And what would you like for whatever upcoming winter holiday you celebrate, little man?"

"Mrrph frmmm phhwahh!" said the little kid, dribbling half-chewed Holidayz HoHoHoles all down Santa Umber's chest.

The kid stuffed another red-and-green-sprinkled HoHoHole in his mouth.

"Maybe you should swallow what you have in your mouth before you talk to Santa," said Santa Umber, flicking the slimy doughnut bits off his red coat.

A very large man, also with a mouthful of Holidayz HoHoHoles, stepped up to Santa and spit out, "Maybe you should mind yer own business and listen to what my kid wants. Yeah?" A big, wet doughnut bit dropped out of the large man's mouth and landed on Umber's black Santa boot with a *plop*.

Santa Umber looked at the doughnut-stuffed man and the doughnut-stuffed kid and thought of a lot of things he could say.

HO HO
HOLES
DUNKER'S

"Yeah?" repeated the man.

"Mrrph frmmm phhwahh!" repeated the kid.

Umber thought, *I have got to get out of here. I have got to get back to being a real AAA agent in good standing. And to do that, I have got to do something amazing to be noticed by the chief.*

"Mrrrrrrph frrrrmmmmm," said the kid, kicking his hard little shoes against Santa Umber's shins.

"Absolutely," Santa Umber answered doughnut man and doughnut boy. "You can count on it. Santa says so."

I have got to do something huge, thought Santa Umber. *I have got to hunt down those aliens I missed and become an AAA hero.*

Santa Umber bounced the doughnut-mouthful kid on his knee, thinking of his plan.

This was a mistake.

Because what Santa Umber did not notice (and could not see) was that the bouncing was shaking up the twenty-four ounces of Mega-Gulp cola that the doughnut kid had guzzled on top of the seven Holidayz HoHoHoles he had snarfed down.

The cola inside the doughnut kid's stomach mixed and fizzed.

Santa Umber bounced his knee, thinking, *SOMETHING BIG!*

The cola inside the doughnut kid's stomach expanded.

Santa Umber bounced his knee, thinking, *SOMETHING AMAZING!*

The cola and half-digested red/green Holidayz HoHoHoles churned and bubbled and pressed upward and outward.

"I've got it!" said Santa Umber, not realizing he was talking out loud.

Santa Umber gave the doughnut kid one last giant bounce on Santa's knee.

And that one last bounce completed Umber's plan . . . and created more pressure than the doughnut kid could hold.

BZZZZZT... OOOPS!

∫ΩΩΩ®† . . . ø ø ø π ß/

The chief locked his door. He pressed a button to lower the long black AAA window shade to cover the far wall of windows. He sat down at his computer. He looked over his shoulder. And then, just as he had every day for the past six weeks, the chief typed in a certain web address.

This page loaded.

This counter filled the screen.

The chief refreshed the spaceheadz.com page. He zoomed in on the counter again to be sure. For the second time that morning someone read the number on the Spaceheadz counter out loud. "Three million one hundred thirty-nine thousand nine hundred and one!"

The three metal paper clips on the chief's desk twitched, then stood on end.

The chief clicked the browser window closed.

The paper clips dropped flat.

The chief examined his AEW monitor. It showed one sharp red peak of a rather large and localized Alien Energy Wave.

"Hmmmm," said the chief. "I wonder who should take care of this mysterious AEW spike?"

The chief absentmindedly chewed the end of an AAA pencil and smiled.

The chief's phone rang. He picked it up and listened. He answered, "Its fleece was white as snow."

Michael K. slalomed down the Ninth Street sidewalk on his SPHDZed skateboard. Venus checked the map on her phone and pedaled her bike right behind Michael K.

"The closest Dunker's is on Fifth Avenue and Seventh Street," called Venus. "It's got to be that one."

"We cannot let the Spaceheadz catch Santa!" yelled Michael K. "If they do, he will know they are aliens in a second. And our whole Spaceheadz Brainwave will be for nothing!"

Michael K. ollied the curb and thanked his lucky stars that he and Venus were at least rolling downhill. Then he started thinking about stars. Then he started thinking about planets. Then he started thinking that Earth was a planet and would get turned off if the Spaceheadz got caught by the AAA. Then Michael K. really started to freak out. He pushed off for more speed, zoomed around a lady pushing a shopping cart, and just missed a man walking a little dog.

Michael K. and Venus zipped around the corner at Fifth Avenue. They flew past Eighth Street.

"Right there!" yelled Venus. "Striped awning on the right."

There was the Dunker's Donuts. A line of people stood behind red velvet ropes.

Michael K. and Venus were still a half a block away. And

Michael K. was just about to say, "I hope we are in time."

He only got as far as "I hope . . ." when the noise of a huge, horrified crowd scream came out of the Dunker's.

"Oh no," said Venus. "That can't be good."

And it wasn't.

Because next the entire crowd of moms and dads and kids and strollers burst out of the Dunker's Donuts and onto the sidewalk, screaming and yelling and moaning and crying.

"Ahhh!" screamed a dad pulling two scared-looking kids behind him.

"Aiieeeee!" yelled a mom running with her little girl in her arms.

As the crowd surged past, Michael K. and Venus fought to work their way inside the doughnut shop.

We were so close, thought Michael K.

A skinny man dressed in some kind of red-white-and-blue underwear ran through the crowd.

"We are too late," Michael K. called to Venus above the screams and yells of the crowd. "Umber must have arrested the Spaceheadz and freaked everyone out."

Venus looked at the panicked crowd all around them.

"Maybe . . . but why does everyone smell so bad?"

In her purple-lit Home Office Control Room, Agent Hot Magenta noticed a very unusual AEW spike.

"Did you see that very unusual AEW spike, Agent Wild Blue Yonder?" said Hot Magenta.

Agent Wild Blue Yonder blinked, then nodded.

"I mean, it's not very unusual that my AEW Detector would detect an AEW," added Hot Magenta. "But look at this location."

Agent Wild Blue Yonder slowly stretched and then stood up.

"Location A-1," whispered Hot Magenta. "How is that possible? That is AAA headquarters!"

Agent Wild Blue Yonder blinked again. She rubbed against Agent Hot Magenta's AAA chair.

"This is Code Ruby Red," said Hot Magenta.

Agent Wild Blue Yonder nodded.

Hot Magenta flipped open her sleek Spaceship-Phone®. She punched one on her speed dial.

"Mary had a little lamb, sir," said Hot Magenta.

She listened to the reply.

"I have recorded a very unusual spike, sir. Location A-1. I repeat—location A-1."

Hot Magenta listened.

"But I designed and built the AEW Detector myself, sir. Like myself, it does not make mistakes."

Hot Magenta listened.

"I can lock this down, sir. I can make this alien arrest right now . . . with no mistakes."

Pause.

"Really, sir? Because I think I—"

Pause.

"And always look up . . . sir."

Agent Hot Magenta clicked her SpaceshipPhone® shut and sat back, just a little bit, in her AAA chair.

"This is so not fair," she said.

Agent Wild Blue Yonder shook her head.

"I am the AAA's top-ranked agent! I have won AAA Agent of the Month for the last twenty-three months! Why is the chief shutting me out like this?"

Hot Magenta tapped and swiped and twisted a flurry of commands on her new custom Virtual 4-D (one more D than 3-D) Keyboard®.

Agent Wild Blue Yonder followed every move.

"Ha!" said Hot Magenta. "Just as I thought. All of my systems are fine. That AEW spike was definitely at A-1. And the way to absolutely confirm it? Get someone in there with my new Gamma Use Meter."

Hot Magenta held up what looked like a pink pack of gum.

Agent Wild Blue Yonder jumped back and batted at a bit of sunlight that reflected off the pack onto the wall.

"Yes," continued Agent Hot Magenta. "But who is that someone?"

Hot Magenta pulled up the home page for antialienagency.com. She logged on to "Agent Buzz" with her password and scanned the names of agents posting.

"Agent Eggplant? Too bossy. Agent Pink Flamingo? Too nosy. Blue Violet? Just plain mean. Jazzberry Jam, no. Mango Tango, no."

Hot Magenta clicked back to "Case Files."

"But there is one agent. The agent involved in the Pizza Problem. The agent in the Dumpster Dive. The agent in the Parent-Teacher Failure.

"Here is the agent the chief keeps picking for every one of these Brooklyn alien missions. Why? He must know something. So the chief won't suspect him if he gets found inside AAA HQ."

Agent Hot Magenta scrolled through her agent phone list in 4-D.

"Agent Umber," said Agent Hot Magenta, and she tapped his number.

Agent Wild Blue Yonder closed her eyes and purred.

Networks

A social network is a connected group of individuals or organizations.

A social network grows bigger and smarter by adding more individuals and more connections.

A social network is kind of like a giant brain.

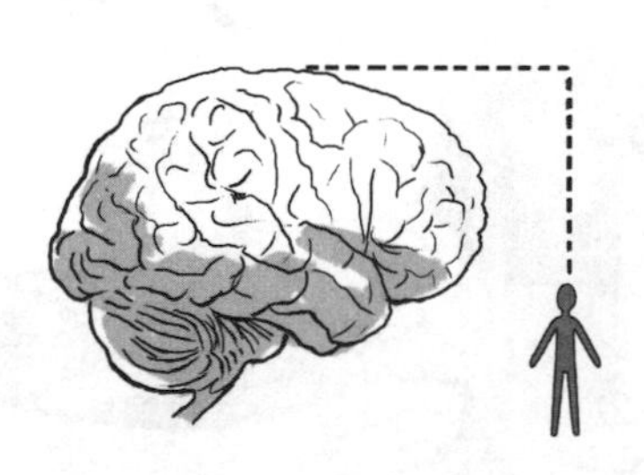

Bob elf, Jennifer elf, and Major Fluffy elf were so close to Santa they could almost touch him.

"Squee week!" said Major Fluffy.

"Oh yes," said Bob. "Because he sees you when you are sleeping. He knows when you're awake. He knows if you've been bad or good. So—"

"We eek, ee eee eee eek," added Major Fluffy.

Jennifer loosened up with a few jumping jacks.

The Spaceheadz elves were so excited by the idea of a man in a red suit making all of their wishes come true that, like Santa himself, they did not notice what was happening with the little doughnut-stuffed boy on Santa's bouncing knee.

The little kid's eyes were bugging out.

Santa bounced his knee.

The little kid's cheeks bulged.

Santa shouted out, "I've got it!"

Santa gave one last bounce with his knee.

Mega-Gulp cola gasses and Holidayz HoHoHoles expanded.

The doughnut-stuffed kid tilted his head back and spewed a geyser of half-digested Holidayz HoHoHoles and sticky brown Mega-Gulp cola up into an overhead ceiling fan.

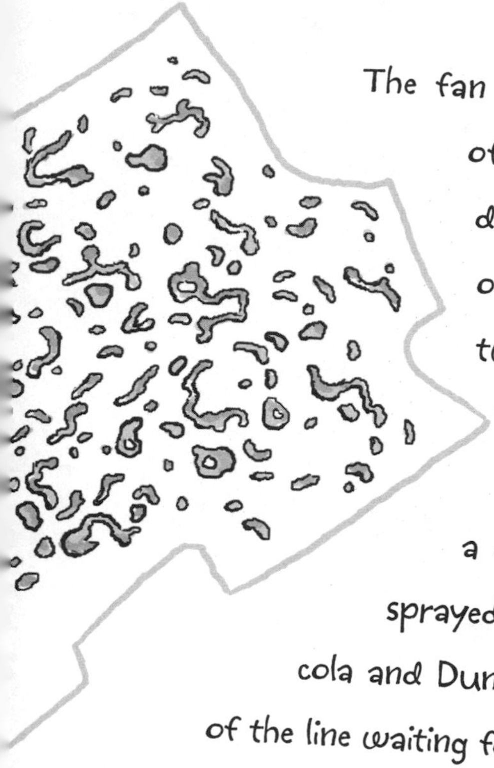

The fan splattered a slimy shower of red-and-green-sprinkled doughnut chunks on everyone and everything within twenty feet of Santa.

Someone screamed.

The doughnut kid took a deep breath . . . and then sprayed another fire-hose blast of cola and Dunker's chunks over the rest of the line waiting for Santa.

The crowd screamed in disgust and horror. Moms and dads grabbed their dripping, crying kids and charged the exit.

"Amazing," said Bob. "I have never seen an Earth person explode like that."

"He forgot to raise his hand," said Jennifer.

More screams. The smelly mob pushed frantically to get out into the open air.

"Eeeek," added Major Fluffy.

The kid took another breath.

Santa jumped up, dumping the barfing kid on the floor. Santa ripped off his upchuck-speckled red coat and pants, and plowed through the screaming, smelly crowd wearing nothing but his Santa hat, his red-white-and-blue AAA long underwear, and his coal black Santa boots.

Bob and Jennifer and Major Fluffy stood dripping in front of Santa's empty chair.

"Eeek eek week," said Major Fluffy.

"You are not kidding," said Bob. "And no pony for me either."

"Now how do we tell Santa our SPHDZ wish?" said Jennifer.

Bob looked around. Bob thought. Bob said, "I think Santa must be playing an Earth game. Like tag."

"Boo-yah!" yelled Jennifer. "Let's catch Santa! Let's catch Santa!"

The disappointed kids took up Jennifer's chant, "Let's catch Santa! Let's catch Santa!"

The moms and dads decided that this must be a new way for their kids to talk to Santa. They had to chase him and catch him. The parents joined in the chant, "LET'S CATCH SANTA! LET'S CATCH SANTA!"

The three urp-covered Spaceheadz elves ran out of Dunker's and right past an openmouthed Michael K. and a nose-covering Venus on the sidewalk outside.

"Come on, Michael K.!" yelled Bob as he sprinted by. "We are going to catch Santa and tell him our wishes!"

A gang of moms, dads, kids, and strollers followed the elves.

It took Michael K.'s brain a second to register what had just happened. It took Michael K.'s brain another second to process what the smelly elf had just yelled.

"NOOOOOOO!" yelled Michael K. after the disappearing elves. "Wait a minute!"

"Michael K. is very funny," said running Jennifer. "He wants us to wait sixty seconds . . . so he can catch Santa and tell him his wish first."

"Ha, ha," laughed Bob in a terrible imitation of a real human laugh. "No way we will wait for sixty seconds."

"Eeee eeee," laughed Major Fluffy.

And the Spaceheadz elves ran even faster toward disaster.

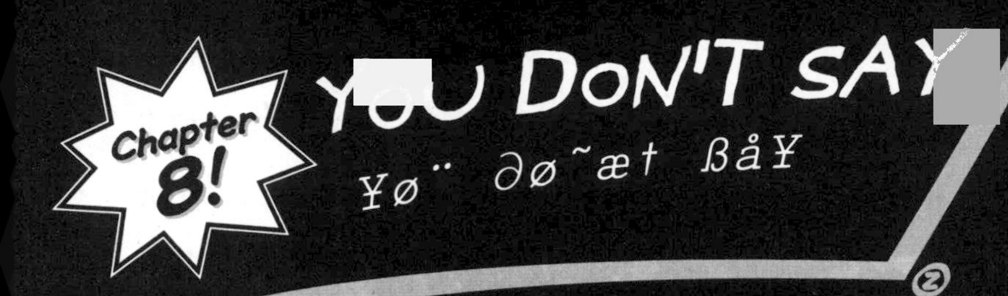

"This could be a complete disaster," said Mom K. She folded the Sunday newspaper and smoothed it out on the kitchen table.

"I know," said Dad K., looking up from the Sports section. "If the Jets don't win today, they might not make the play-offs!"

"No," said Mom K. "I'm talking about all this mind control." Mom K. tapped her finger on an article. "Neuromarketing, they are calling it. Companies and governments are making people want what they are told to want. You want this toilet paper. You want to elect Joe Schmo. It's using people's brains in ways they don't even know."

Mom K. was going to tell Dad K. about the work her ZIA agency was doing tracking some of these mind control projects around the globe. But she had gotten word from her boss, just yesterday, that every bit of this work was top secret.

"Uh, yeah," said Dad K., nervously hiding his face behind the page of sports news.

Dad K. was going to tell Mom K. about his project with DarkWave X. And how it was using advertising to "help shape people's thinking." And how they were going to test the IWANT Pulsar maybe even this week. But he had gotten word from one of those big, quiet guys in the dark blue suits, just yesterday, that every bit of this work was beyond top secret.

The DarkWave X IWANT Pulsar was so secret, said the guy in the blue suit, that if Dad K. even thought too much about it, he would be sorry. Very sorry.

"Groo?" Baby K. asked Dad K.

"I think if they just throw the ball a little more, mix things up with some pass plays, they'll be fine," said Dad K.

"Goo gah," said Baby K.

This mind control article reminded Mom K. about the project that her ZIA Task Force was tracking. Something about a wave. And an X. She should get online now. Check it out. It was turning into something big.

But first she turned the newspaper page.

"Oh, and look," said Mom K. "Santa is going to be at the Dunker's Donuts from twelve to three today. Does Baby want to go see Santa?"

Both Baby K. and Dad K. looked terrified.

"Nooo tay," said Baby K. "Nooo bah bah tay."

Chapter 9! YODEL BELLS

¥ø∂´¬ ∫´¬¬ß

"Yodel-ay-eee-hoo! Yodel-ay-eee-hoo!" rang Agent Umber's Picklephone®.

Umber had forgotten to set it on vibrate. And he had accidentally picked the yodeling ringtone.

How embarrassing.

Again.

Agent Umber unclipped his Picklephone® from the waistband of his AAA underwear.

"There he is!" yelled the large, angry man behind him.

Umber kept running as fast as his Santa boots would let him, and checked the ID on the incoming call.

No way! She was one of the very best agents in the whole AAA. Why was she calling?

Umber answered his Picklephone® . . . and accidentally also activated his new videophone option.

"Little Bo Peep has lost her sheep," said Agent Hot Magenta.

Oops. Magenta popped up on the little Picklescreen®.

Umber answered very coolly, "And can't tell where to find them."

"Agent Umber," said Agent Hot Magenta. "The AAA needs you. I need you."

Umber tripped on a crack in the sidewalk and stumbled, spinning around in a circle.

Agent Hot Magenta said she needed him! She was so smart. She was so cool. She was so AAA.

Umber flapped his arms around to regain his balance and kept running.

"Of course you do," answered Umber.

"Why are you spinning your videophone around?" said Hot Magenta. "Stop it. You are making me dizzy."

"Stop that Santa!" yelled one of the moms in the crowd rolling after Umber.

"Did you just call me Santa?" said Agent Hot Magenta.

Umber held his Picklephone® close, filling the screen with his giant face.

"I said 'I'm on the case like Santa!'" Umber yelled into his Picklephone®.

Umber jumped over a kid's toy stroller on

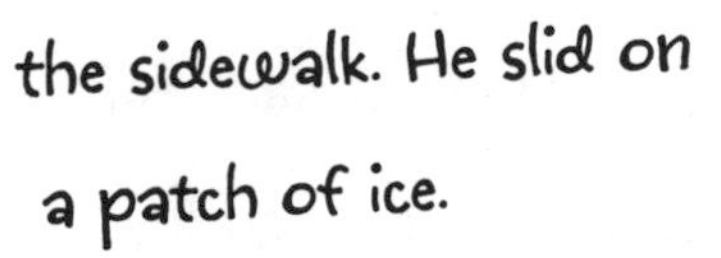

the sidewalk. He slid on a patch of ice.

"That makes no sense," said the little video screen image of Agent Hot Magenta. "Where are you? And what is all of that red, white, and blue I'm seeing?"

"Rahr! Rahr! Rahr!" yelled the angry crowd chasing Umber.

Umber slipped, bounced off a tree, and kept running.

"In the middle . . . of . . . evasive . . . maneuvers . . . ," Umber managed to huff out.

"Right," said Agent Hot Magenta. "Meet me at the Secret Spot at eighteen hundred tonight. I've got a Code Ruby Red . . . if you can handle it."

The Secret Spot? A Ruby Red? Umber was thrilled. "You can count on Agent Umber," said Agent Umber.

"And Agent Umber?"

"Yes?"

"You better pick up your pace. Those elves are gaining on you."

Umber looked over his shoulder to check the elves.

Which might explain why he never saw the open sewer main.

On her SpaceshipPhone® video Agent Hot Magenta saw another flash of red, white, and blue . . . gray sky . . . darkness . . . then nothing.

Networks II

If electrical activity in the brain's network forms thoughts and ideas,

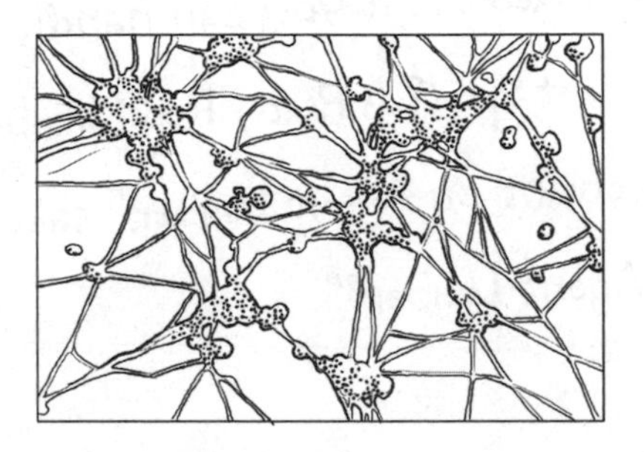

what does activity in a social network shape?

Social thoughts? Social ideas?

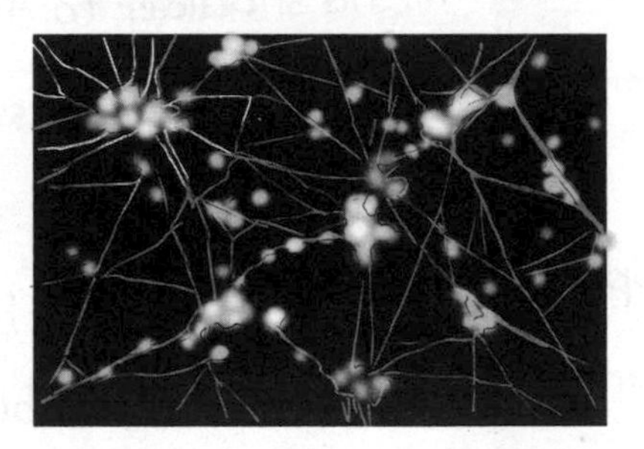

Michael K. raced down the sidewalk, carving around kids, parents, strollers, and dogs like they were obstacles in a video game.

Venus pedaled behind him, following his line.

Bob elf and Jennifer elf ran after the skinny man in the Santa hat and long underwear, leading a small crowd of angry, smelly Dunker's Donuts customers.

"Bob and Jennifer, stop!" yelled Michael K., swerving around a garbage can.

Bob and Jennifer looked back and waved at Michael K. and Venus. "We will catch Santa Claus first!" they yelled back. And they kept running.

"That is not who you think it is!"

Bob and Jennifer ran even faster. They were closing in on the gangly runner wearing the Santa hat and Santa boots and not much else. And now it looked like Santa was talking to a pickle.

That could not be good.

Michael K. leaned down and pushed off with one more burst of speed. It was all or nothing now.

"That is not Santa Claus! It's Agent Umber dressed up to look like Santa Claus!"

That worked.

Bob and Jennifer stopped so fast that both Michael K. and Venus crashed into them and made a huge pileup of elves and kids and board and bike.

"Eeeeeeek!"

And hamster.

"Eee eeek weeek eek eeek."

Make that "and leader of the Spaceheadz, Major Fluffy."

Bob elf sat up, looking stunned. "That is not Santa Claus?"

"No," said Venus, untangling her leg from her crashed bike. "That is Agent Umber, AAA."

"That is very not wholesome freshness," said Jennifer. "How can he do that?"

"Eee weee eeek," added Major Fluffy from the bottom of the pile.

Michael K. decided he really needed to scare Bob and Jennifer to keep them away from Umber.

"That Santa is bad," said Michael K. "If you catch him, Santa will destroy the world."

Michael K. was so intent on scaring Bob and Jennifer that he didn't notice the crowd of Dunker's moms and dads and little kids who had caught up to them.

A little kid in an orange stroller instantly started crying, "Whaaaa! Santa is bad!"

Two more kids started wailing, "Whaaa! Santa is going to destroy the world!"

Michael K. and Venus untangled themselves and pulled Bob and Jennifer to their feet.

"What's wrong with you?" asked a large, angry man holding one of the criers. "Why would you say a thing like that?"

Now Michael K. and Venus and the Spaceheadz were surrounded by a circle of crying kids and angry parents.

"Shame on you kids . . ."

"No respect . . ."

"Just mean . . ."

Michael K. looked around. Santa Umber had disappeared. Completely.

"WHAAAAA!" yelled one kid, louder than everyone else. "I want my F-18 Hornet fighter jet! WHAAAAA!"

Michael K. backed away from the crowd, pulling Venus and the Spaceheadz with him.

"We would really like to stay and explain all of this," said Michael K., "but we really have to . . . RUN!"

And they did.

HO, HO, HO

Safely inside the Spaceheadz' house, Bob and Jennifer and Major Fluffy fed on video from their array of screens while they asked Michael K. questions.

"So other persons sometimes make themselves look like Santa?" said Bob.

"Yes," said Michael K.

"But they are not Santa," said Jennifer.

"No," said Michael K.

"Eeeek?" said Major Fluffy.

Michael K. didn't have his Fluffy translator, so he shrugged.

Bob and Jennifer and Major Fluffy thought about this for a moment.

Finally Bob said, "This is very strange. And not

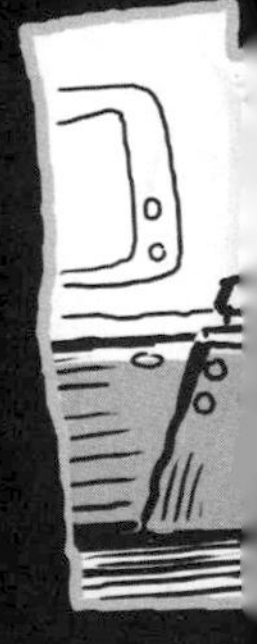

Naturally Flavored. But everything you tell us, Michael K., we believe."

Venus whispered behind Michael K., "Do not get started on the Tooth Fairy or the Easter Bunny."

"Ho, ho, ho," said Michael K. "Ho, ho, ho."

"We'll see you in class tomorrow," said Venus.

And she got Michael K. out of there before he said anything else.

Back in the living room, Mom K. sat on the couch and flipped open her gunmetal gray ZIA laptop. She opened the fake hairtodaystyles.com website. She selected her secret key settings:

Stylist: Chrissy

What do you need: Styling

Date: 1/23

Time: 4:56

Mom K. clicked on th top of the spray can nozzle. The Hair Today website sli up and revealed the secret ZI website behind it.

Dad K. sat in his leather chair on the other side of the living room.

On his fake-brick-covered Ad Factory iPad he scrolled through his DarkWave X files.

This was big.

This was huge.

This could happen any minute now.

Dad K. reread his last e-mail from the DarkWave X team.

To: Top Eyes Only

From: DWX

IWANT Pulsar nearly fully powered.

Stand by for test firing notice.

Baby K. sat in the middle of the couch, surrounded by her stuffed teddy bears, her plush ponies, and her famous-scientist action figures.

Baby K. put Nikola Tesla on the back of the pink Dream Wind pony and galloped them over the plaid pillow mountains. Tesla stopped Dream Wind to talk to Marie Curie, riding Fuzzy Panda.

"Goo gah goo," said Albert Einstein.

"Gah gah goo gar," answered Marie Curie.

On the big-screen TV, one of the giant figures in a green-and-white outfit and matching helmet threw a funny-shaped ball up in the air. The ball flew down the length of the white-striped rectangle of grass. One of the other green-and-white helmeted figures jumped up and caught the ball.

Eighty thousand people sitting in rows around the rectangle of space, most of them also wearing the same green-and-white numbered shirts as the action figures, jumped up screaming and clapping and cheering.

"Yeah!" said Dad K.

Mom K. opened her ZIA Top Level Alerts.

Bad news.

1. Due to possible bad reactions, there will be no more chocolate peanut butter cups at lunch.

2. The secret DarkWave X project we have been tracking is going to be tested soon. We don't know when or where.

Ping.

Dad K. read his incoming e-mail.

IWANT Pulsar test firing 1500. Location 42/08. Top level.

Ping.

Mom K. read her incoming e-mail.

Test tomorrow at 3 p.m. We still don't know where. We don't know what. We do know it is brain control. And it is big.

Michael K. slammed the front door shut behind him. He dropped his skateboard in the front hall. He dropped his backpack on the living-room floor.

"Hey. What's up?"

Mom K. and Dad K. both jumped in surprise.

"Nothing!" said both Mom K. and Dad K. at exactly the same time.

"Goo gah gah gah, go gooo goo goo," explained Baby K.

Eighty thousand people surrounding a green rectangle of white-striped grass groaned.

Group Intelligence

A flock of birds, a swarm of bees, a herd of buffalo, and a school of fish are all organized in the same way.

They do not have any one leader.

The group decides where to go and how to avoid predators together, with a group mind.

So if you went up to a buffalo and said, "Take me to your leader," he would have to take you to the whole herd.

Umber could not believe he was actually meeting with Agent Hot Magenta at **THE SECRET SPOT.**

He had read her posts on antialien agency.com for years.

She was the best.

Now she needed his help.

And **THE SECRET SPOT** was the very coolest place to meet, because **THE SECRET SPOT** had . . .

. . . the best bagels in the whole city.

Agent Umber smiled coolly. This was cool. He was cool. He had lost those crazy elf kids chasing him by coolly falling in an open sewer pipe. Now he had a cool bump on his head and was coolly meeting the coolest agent in the whole—

". . . clear?" said Agent Hot Magenta.

She was looking at him.

He must have missed a sentence or two when she was talking and he was being cool.

Agent Hot Magenta leaned forward over the little table and repeated, "Is that clear?"

Agent Umber had no idea what she had just said.

Agent Umber leaned forward too.

Agent Umber said, "Yes."

"Very good," said Agent Hot Magenta. She handed Umber a small pink-purple pack of GUM. She nodded.

Agent Umber took it and nodded back.

He coolly took a bite of his pumpernickel bagel and, with his mouth still full, said, "Lehhr juh gah roh roh rah deed ah wuh mo tah."

Agent Hot Magenta stared at Agent Umber. She began to think that maybe this wasn't such a good idea after all. "Pardon?"

Agent Umber swallowed his bagel bite and coughed.

"Sorry. I was, uh . . . speaking in code." Umber looked around the otherwise empty bagel shop. "I said, 'Let's go over the details one more time.'"

"Get into AAA HQ, record everything you can at the spike location, A-1, and get out," said Agent Hot Magenta.

"Right," said Agent Umber. "And how am I going to do that?"

"With the GUM recorder I just handed to you."

"Right," said Umber, picking up the pack of gum.

"GUM is short for Gamma Use Meter. It records any traces of alien activity."

"I knew that," said Umber.

Hot Magenta shook her head. "You should have exactly twenty-two minutes. Everyone will be at the AAA holiday party."

Umber nodded coolly. "I bet you got that secret intelligence from a wireless Flower Vase Tap®, then decoded it with your Coffee Grinder Decoder®."

Agent Hot Magenta paused. "No. We all got the holiday party Evite. You click on the blue-colored link. Like this."

Hot Magenta brought up the link on her phone, clicked it, and showed Umber the invitation.

"Right," said Umber. "You click on the blue-colored link. I always do that."

"Scan the entire location with the GUM pack. That will give us all the alien info we need."

This is so cool, thought Agent Umber. *I am working with Agent Hot Magenta. Nothing can stop me now. I am the best agent ever. I will be the coolest agent to ever catch aliens and clear the Umber family name and—*

". . . clear?" said Agent Hot Magenta, standing up. She was looking at him.

Umber paused for just a second and, even though he was not at all completely clear, answered, "Right."

FROSTY

f®øßt¥

Monday afternoon Mrs. Halley said, "Well, we certainly have made some . . . unusual . . . holiday dioramas this morning."

Mrs. Halley looked at the shoe boxes showing scenes of everything from the usual Santas and shepherds to the unusual jet fighters, dinosaurs, whales, Peeps, elephants, and ants.

"The most . . . unusual . . . I have ever seen in all my years. . . ."

She tried very hard, but not very successfully, not to frown.

"I will put these on our Mrs. Halley's Comets dot com website tonight. And we will hear about everyone's different holidays tomorrow during our 501-B holiday party and show-and-tell."

Venus nudged Michael K. and TJ and showed them her phone.

Michael K. and TJ high-fived.

Mrs. Halley looked at the Peeps listening to a hamster. She looked at the elephants walking around a volcano. She seemed to remember something about someone's holiday with an elephant but had no idea what could be going on with the bunny Peeps and the hamster. "It will be especially interesting to hear about the holidays celebrated by Bob and Michael K."

Bob waved to all of room 501-B.

Michael K. slid down low in his seat.

"And I know we had talked about bringing in holiday food from all lands for our party . . . ," Mrs. Halley continued.

Venus, Michael K., TJ, Bob, and Jennifer huddled around Venus's phone in the back of the classroom.

". . . but this year I was thinking I might just bring in my Frosty the Snowman cookies."

The Spaceheadz counter rolled over to

Red, white, and blue digital fireworks exploded across the Spaceheadz web page.

filled the screen.

Venus, Michael K., TJ, Bob, and Jennifer cheered. Major Fluffy eeek-squeaked and did a backflip.

"Goodness," said Mrs. Halley.

And if you had been sitting in the front row of room 501-B, you might have seen Mrs. Halley actually blushing. "Kids do love my Frosty the Snowman cookies. But I didn't know you loved them this much."

Venus and Michael K. and TJ and Bob and Jennifer cheered and hugged and jumped around.

"Only ten more Spaceheadz to go!" cheered Venus.

Mrs. Halley smiled. The new children this year were the strangest fifth graders she had ever seen. But at least they knew good cookies when they tasted them.

Venus's phone flashed a giant **10**

Group Intelligence II

Group intelligence works great when it helps a flock of birds fly south for the winter, or a school of fish escape a hungry shark.

But a large bunch of people acting as a group may sometimes do things an individual would not have done on his or her own. This is sometimes called, not surprisingly, herd mentality.

Crowds rioting, stock markets crashing, and sports fans going nuts are sometimes the result of herd mentality.

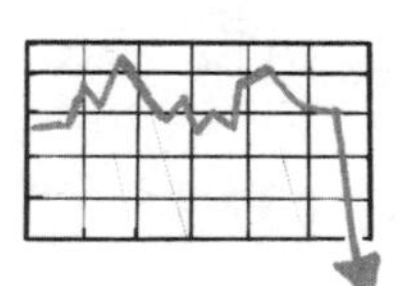

HARD-BOILED

·å®∂-ʃø^¬´∂

In a secret office, hidden behind the giant underwear billboard in the middle of Times Square, Dad K. sat at a table with two men and one woman. All three wore the same shiny blue suits. And all three had introduced themselves using only code names.

The man called Delta clicked a remote and powered up a video display that covered the entire far wall of the room.

The woman called Foxtrot pointed her finger at the display and moved a red arrow on-screen.

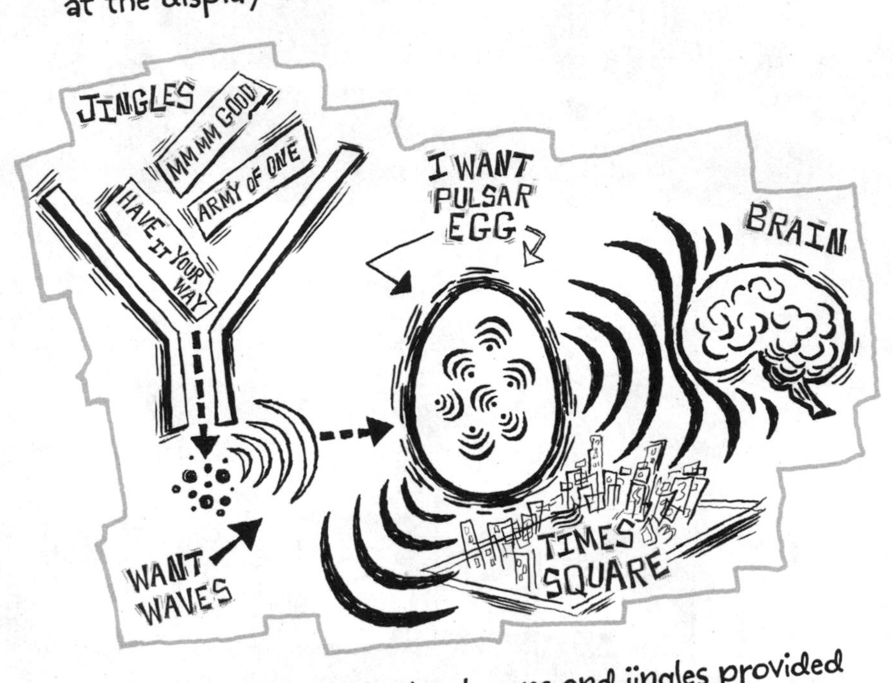

"So. To review: The slogans and jingles provided by Mr. K.—here—have been distilled and concentrated as WantWaves—here. . . ."

The man called Echo took over the pointer and continued the explanation of the diagram, pointing at a blinking black egg shape on the screen.

"We have loaded the WantWaves into our IWANT Pulsar—here—positioned it just above us over Times Square—here. . . ."

Foxtrot took over. "The IWANT Pulsar will send the WantWaves out over the test subjects in Times Square. The waves stimulate the WANT center of the subjects' brains—here. . . ."

Echo continued. "The test subjects should then WANT what we have programmed them to want."

Foxtrot finished. "For this test we have shaped the charge for the victims . . . I mean subjects . . . to WANT Purple Nertz.

"What the heck are Purple Nertz?" said Dad K.

"Nothing," said Foxtrot. "They don't exist. This way we know, when subjects ask for them, that they have been affected by our WantWave."

Dad K. sat back in his chair. This was all news to him. He thought he had just been sending DarkWave X slogans and jingles for a new product.

"I don't know," said Dad K. "This doesn't sound exactly safe to me. Shouldn't we be trying this on mice or rabbits or something first?"

"Great idea," said Delta. "If we wanted to control mice and rabbits."

Echo and Foxtrot laughed.

Dad K. looked at all of the people swarming around the streets of Times Square.

"But these people don't know we are doing this. Isn't this against some kind of law?"

"We are the law," said Delta.

This did not seem like a good answer to Dad K. He decided it was time to get out of this shady project.

"Well, okay then. I guess you've got everything you need from me."

Dad K. stood up to leave.

Echo put one meaty hand on Dad K.'s shoulder and pushed him back down into his seat. "Oh, no, ad guy. You are part of the DarkWave X team now. And you stay part of the team until we say you are not part of the team."

Dad K. felt sick. "So you are really going to Want-Wave all of those unsuspecting people?"

"No," said Foxtrot. "*We* are going to WantWave all of those unsuspecting people."

Delta positioned a giant red button on the screen.

Echo pulled out a box of aluminum foil. He tore off

a sheet, wrapped it around his head, then tore off sheets for Delta, Foxtrot, and Dad K.

"The waveproof helmets didn't make it in time. So I got the heavy-duty extra-wide. ***KEEPS THE FRESHNESS INSIDE.***"

Delta and Foxtrot wrapped their aluminum foil around their heads.

It would have been funny if it weren't so scary.

"Starting IWANT Pulsar countdown," said Foxtrot. She clicked the giant red button.

The video displayed a huge counter.

A robotic voice intoned, "Twenty . . . nineteen . . ."

Dad K. stared at the piece of aluminum foil in his hand. This seemed wrong. He didn't want to be part of this.

"Eighteen . . . seventeen . . ."

But he was part of this.

"Sixteen . . . fifteen . . ."

Dad K. wrapped the aluminum foil around his head.

Agent Umber crouched in the Ready Tiger position.

He bowed to his partner.

"This is it, Agent Speedy. All these years of AAA training and AAA practice. It all comes down to this."

Agent Speedy nodded silently.

"Karate, judo, kung fu, muay thai, krav maga, Mortal Kombat, kendo, sushi, hula . . ."

Umber warmed up with a couple of jumping jacks.

His windmilling hand flipped his plate of toast on the floor. He bent down to pick it up and smacked his head on the chair.

"Oooh!"

Umber spun a back kick at the chair. His foot poked through the rungs, and he fell on one knee.

"Ahhh!"

Umber untangled himself from the chair, slipped on the rug, and fell flat on his back.

"Yow!"

Agent Speedy didn't move.

Agent Umber stood up very slowly, very carefully.

"I'm going into AAA HQ, Speedy. One shot. One chance. This is how it's done—AAA agent Umber style!"

Umber jumped from a standing start into a full Leaping Lizard over the bed. He 360-Typhoon twisted and formed an Earthquake Hammer Fist.

Agent Speedy stood perfectly still.

Like he was moving in slow motion, Agent Umber caught the tip of his shoe on his bedspread.

Umber's spinning motion twisted the cloth around his ankles and pulled his feet backward as the momentum of his Earthquake Hammer Fist moved his upper body forward.

Umber smashed against his apartment wall with two mighty thuds.

First his fist.

Then his head.

Umber slid down the wall and crumpled into the

little space between his bed and the wall. His eyes were closed. But he wasn't completely unconscious. He was ready to take on his biggest mission, or at least as ready as he would ever be.

Agent Umber groaned, "Ooh!"

Agent Speedy took a bite of lettuce.

Agent Speedy nodded.

Group Intelligence III

The Internet is kind of like a swarm or flock or herd.

It does not have a single leader.

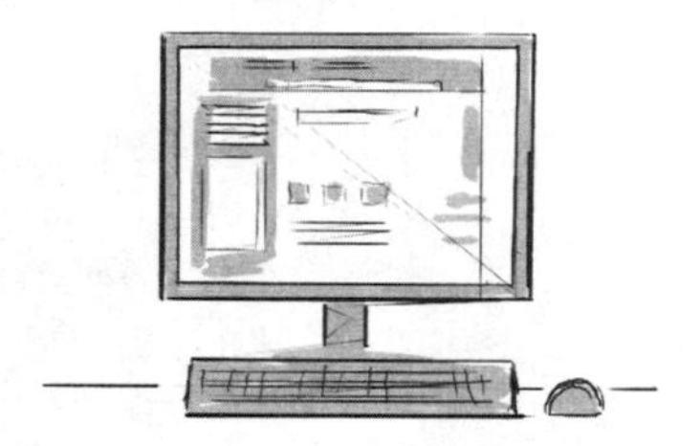

It is made of individual pieces that can be linked.

Maybe it should change its name to the World Wide Herd, the World Wide Flock, or the World Wide Swarm?

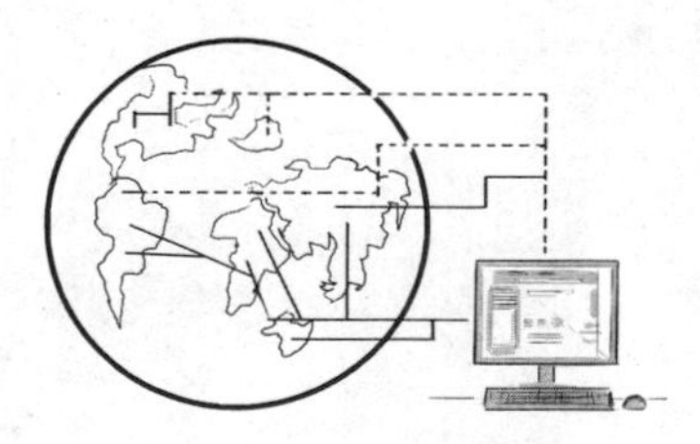

3, 2, 1, SPHDZ

£≤ ™≤ ¡≤ ßπ˙∂Ω

Venus's phone showed

5

"And maybe I will make my elf cupcakes," continued Mrs. Halley.

4

"Yes!" said Michael K.

Mrs. Halley smiled. "And reindeer gumdrops."

3

"Yes!" said Venus.

Mrs. Halley, now completely inspired, starting writing her new holiday party menu on the board.

"Candy canes."

2

"Yes! Yes!" said Bob.

"Gingerbread men!" said Mrs. Halley.

1

"Yes! Yes! Yes!" said Jennifer.

Mrs. Halley paused. Her eyes lit up.

"And my family recipe . . . All Holiday Fruitcake!"

SPHDZ mission accomplished.

"YEAH!!!!!!!!!!!!!!"

cheered Bob and Jennifer and Venus and TJ and Michael K.

"All-natural ultra-strength three point one four million and one Brainwave!" cheered Bob.

Mrs. Halley beamed. Strangest children ever.

"You did it, Michael K.," said Venus. "You helped the Spaceheadz save the world. Not bad for a kind of nerdy fifth grader."

Michael K. blushed. He was so thrilled and relieved he didn't know what to say. So he gave Venus an awkward hug. And then blushed some more.

"Eeek eeek squeee eeek!" cheered Major Fluffy.

All of room 501-B joined in the cheering and celebration . . . without really knowing why.

PULSE

Π¨¬ß´

"Fourteen . . . thirteen . . ."

Dad K. tucked his aluminum foil dome behind his ear. He tried to think of some way to stop this disaster.

"Hey, team. I think I just came up with a better slogan we should add in before we try this."

"Twelve . . . eleven . . ."

Something slammed outside the secret-office door. The sound of footsteps rang on the iron stairs.

"We could maybe run it by a focus group?"

"Ten . . . nine . . ."

Someone, something, was battering the office door. Before Delta, Echo, and Foxtrot could even stand up, the door exploded in.

"Everyone freeze! ZIA!"

"Eight . . . seven . . ."

A swarm of ZIA agents in dark green Windbreakers with giant white ZIA letters on front and back piled into the office.

"Six . . . five . . ."

The DarkWave X team stood up with their hands out, showing they were not armed or dangerous.

The ZIA team leader walked into the room.

"Four . . ."

Dad K. was shocked to see that the ZIA team leader was Mom K.

"Three . . ."

The ZIA team leader, Mom K., scanned the four perps who were for some reason wearing aluminum foil hats.

"Two . . ."

Mom K. was shocked to see that one of the perps was Dad K.

"One . . ."

"Honey?" said Mom K.

"Sweetie?" said Dad K.

"Pulse."

The image of the counter clicked to a flat line.

The image of the black egg shape wobbled and sent out segments of black waves.

The WantWaves started at the IWANT Pulsar and spread like ripples from a stone thrown into a pond. A pond that was all of Times Square . . . and the thousands of unsuspecting people in it.

BRAIN FREEZE

∫®å^~ ƒ®´´Ω´

Room 501-B hummed with the excitement of

1. two minutes left in the last period of the day
2. only one more half day before Winter Break
3. the Spaceheadz saving the world

"I'm gonna sleep in every morning and watch cartoons all day," said Joey.

"I am going to make special holiday cards with my family," said Lisa.

"You are a loser," said Joey.

Venus and Michael K. put on their coats and packed up their books.

"What are you going to do, now that you don't have to save the world anymore?" said Venus.

Michael K. sat down at his desk and leaned back with his hands behind his head.

"Michael K. can do anything," said Bob.

"Weeek eeek," said Major Fluffy.

Jennifer put on her new NASCAR jacket. "He is ***RAM TOUGH***."

"I don't know," said Michael K. "I think I might just do nothing. It's kind of a good feeling. And that was a very cool countdown screen you designed for the three point one four million plus one Brainwave."

Venus pulled out her phone and admired the blinking Spaceheadz screen. "Thanks. I thought we deserved something flashy."

But Michael K. and Venus had hardly a minute to enjoy their success.

"Oh, no," said Bob. "Look!"

Michael K. jumped to his feet. "What? What?"

Bob pointed out the window. "Your Earth clouds are falling down."

"Oh, man," said Michael K. "Don't freak us out like that. It's called snow. Remember we talked about that? You scared me. For a second there I thought you were going to tell us some terrible Spaceheadz surprise."

"Oh, no," said Jennifer. "Look!"

"Snow," said Bob, now that he was an expert.

But Jennifer was not pointing out the window. She was pointing at the Spaceheadz counter on Venus's phone.

Everyone looked.

"Why are the numbers going backward?" said TJ.

Venus tapped the screen and tried to reload the page. "I don't know. I didn't program anything like this."

"This is probably just some kind of Spaceheadz thing, right, Jennifer?" said Michael K. "Like maybe once the Brainwave is complete, it gets downloaded by General Accounting? And then we all get a medal or a prize or something?"

Jennifer wired her GI Joe into Venus's phone and tried to stop the dwindling numbers. "No. Something bad is happening. Someone is taking the Brainwave."

The first dismissal bell rang.

Most of 501-B headed out the door and happily down the stairs. Three nervous Earth persons and three nervous Spaceheadz stayed, staring at a small screen.

Jennifer's GI Joe buzzed. Jennifer replied, "Beep?"

GI Joe responded, "Beez beep beep boop."

Jennifer twisted GI Joe's head. GI Joe spoke in computer-accented English.

"Best greetings to you human persons and SPHDZ. This is General Accounting. Thanks you for collecting the three point one four million plus one Brainwave. I am now stealing it for one very evil plan to bllrrp the planet Gonf. Ha, ha, ha."

"What?" said Michael K. "No way! This is our Brainwave. We are using it to keep Earth from getting turned off! And what is 'bllrrp the planet Gonf,' anyway?"

Jennifer shook her head. "It means destroy every living thing on Gonf and make it into . . . your word, I think is—parking lot."

The numbers on the Spaceheadz counter whizzed backward faster and faster.

"My Wave Collector is on your planet," continued GI Joe/General Accounting. "We could not do it without your help. Thanks you, SPHDZ. Thanks you, Michael K."

"What?" said Michael K. "This is crazy. This is terrible. You can't use our Brainwave to destroy a planet and make it a . . . a . . . parking lot!"

"They can't do this," said Venus.

Everyone stared at the Spaceheadz counter as it clicked to zero and broke in half.

"Ha, ha, ha," said GI Joe, and he clicked off.

"This can't be happening," said Venus. "Wait! I'll check our admin recording." Venus clicked SPHDZ ADMIN at the bottom right corner of the spaceheadz.com page. She entered her VENUS password. They all gathered around Venus's phone and re-watched the sight of the 3.14 + 1 celebration . . . and the awful draining to zero. "This is happening," said Venus. "It happened."

Michael K. turned to Bob and Jennifer and Major Fluffy. "What did you do? You were just using me to collect your Spaceheadz Brainwave. And now it's going to be used to do something really terrible!"

The final dismissal bell rang.

"No!" said Bob.

"We did not know this!" said Jennifer.

"Week eek!" said Major Fluffy.

"We must stop General Accounting," said Bob. "He is SPHDZ gone bad. You must help us get back the Brainwave, Michael K."

Michael K. grabbed his backpack.

"That sounds a lot like something I heard before. I'm not going to get fooled again."

Michael K. walked out the door. In five seconds his world had gone from the best day ever to the worst day in the whole universe.

And now he had had enough. He had been tricked. And then he had helped trick 3.14 million other suckers!

He was done fixing other people's messes.

Done.

Chapter 20! HO, HO, NO

If you were on the Lower East Side of Manhattan, right above Chinatown, on a certain winter afternoon not too long ago . . . you might have seen what you thought was a UUPS delivery guy walk into a corner deli and order a meatball sub with extra sauce.

What you actually saw was Agent Umber, disguised as a UUPS delivery guy, using the meatball-sub password to slip into one of the many secret AAA HQ entrances.

Umber took his meatball sub, nodded to the counterman, and stepped through the scuffed-up white door in the back.

A large lady burst out of the bathroom stall and screamed at him, "Get out of here, you creep!"

Umber got out of there as fast as he could.

Umber stepped through a second scuffed-up white door right next to first scuffed-up white door. The one that didn't have the on it.

Darkness. A number pad glowing with a faint blue light.

Umber tucked the meatball sub under one arm and typed in Hot Magenta's Three Blind Mice code:

The metal door popped open with a surprising metal *THUNK!*

Surprised, Umber dropped his meatball sub in the darkness and dived through the doorway before it closed. He was in! Meatball-sub-less . . . but in.

Umber scooped up his fake delivery package, straightened his brown UUPS hat, and walked down the brightly lit hallway with confidence, like he knew where he was going.

He didn't.

Umber took a right, a left, a right, a right, and another left, a left, a right, a right, a left, straight, a left, a right, down the hall another bit, and one more left.

Umber found himself standing in front of a row of offices that looked just like the row of offices he had walked past ten minutes ago.

He had no idea how to find the chief's office now.

BZZZRT.

Umber's Picklephone® text alert buzzed. He checked the screen. Agent Hot Magenta.

R U IN? YR SIGNAL IS WANDERING IN CIRCLES.
USE YR GPS TO LOCATE SPOT A-1.

Umber texted back:

RIGHT. I KNEW THAT.
ALMOST THERE.

Hot Magenta replied:

HURRY UP.
OFCE PARTY BREAKING UP EARLY.

Umber fumbled with his Picklephone®. He could never remember which hidden button did what on this stupid phone.

Umber tapped what he thought was the hidden GPS bump on his pickle.

A blast of salsa-music ringtone rocked the empty hallway.

Umber tried to switch it off but only managed to cycle through bells, buzzers, heavy-metal guitar, and a rooster crowing before somehow hitting the mute bump.

Umber hid behind the olive green file cabinet and peeked around the corner. Nothing. Yet. He realized he better get cracking.

Umber punched another pickle bump. The screen popped on. That was it. No, maybe not. What was that little red blinking light? Why was it showing a shoe? Why was it showing his shoe?

"Ahh, snicker bits!" cursed Umber. "It's the video function."

Umber smacked the pickle against his forehead in frustration.

The GPS screen popped up.

"Aha," said Umber. "Right."

The GPS screen showed the red destination flag

marking the chief's office right next to the pulsing blue light of Umber's location. But Umber didn't see a door or office anywhere in the long hallway.

Umber stepped back and bumped a large framed portrait of J. Edgar Hoover, the first director of the FBI. The whole section of wall with the portrait spun open. It was exactly the same, portrait and all, on both sides. Umber fell into a hidden office.

"Aha," said Umber. "Right."

The wall continued spinning and sealed shut.

The dim blue gray light of the large screens covering one whole wall lit the office in a spooky glow. There was an AAA office chair, cranked up high to reach the desk. A phone that looked like a spider, or maybe an ant. A nameplate on the desk that said it all:

Umber had done it. He was in the heart of the AAA HQ. The very spot where the AEW spike had spiked.

Umber jumped into action. He ripped open the fake package. He pulled out Agent Hot Magenta's GUM recorder. He hit record.

And for the first time in Agent Umber's life, everything actually worked just like it was supposed to.

The record light started blinking.

Umber stood at attention and saluted the giant AAA seal on the chief's wall.

This was going to make history.

He was finally going to catch the aliens, become a hero, and make up for everything that had ever happened to his family name.

Umber thought, *This is too good to be true.*

And that's when he heard someone on the other side of the chief's secret wall say, "Ho, ho, ho."

Agent Umber quickly calculated that it was probably not Santa Claus.

Agent Umber dived under the chief's desk and made himself as small as possible.

In Times Square lights flashed, horns honked, people swarmed everywhere.

Gigantic letters blinked a spastic barrage of color and light, screaming Canon, Samsung, Coca-Cola, Suntory, Boss McDonald's Toshiba Cinnabon Hilton Applebee's Sony Starbucks Toshiba AMC Theatres Carvel Kodak Car of the Year Hershey's No Turns Loews Olympus *Grease* Foot Locker TDK Mountain Dew *The Lion King* Panasonic One Way JVC Sbarro TKTS Swatch *Stomp* Rock Band Bank of America Subway Geico Yahoo! Target Aquos Chase Maxell Levi's Pepsi LG Toys "R" Us *Eyewitness News* ABC MTV AT&T and more more more.

SAMSUNG
SWATCH
ABC
SONY
TODAY IS
COLA
TKTS
CANON
GREASE

Crowds of people stampeded north and south, east and west, streaming over sidewalks, across streets, out of doors, in and out of subway tunnels.

A completely green woman stood frozen on a box with one arm raised.

A man wearing only his underwear and cowboy boots played a guitar.

A bearded old guy in a long black coat yelled, "The end is here!"

In other words—everything was completely normal.

Delta, Echo, and Foxtrot climbed up into a giant black SUV with tinted windows waiting at the curb.

The ZIA agents and Dad K. stood on the sidewalk.

Delta slammed the SUV door and rolled down the window.

"Thanks for the help, adman."

The SUV roared away from the curb and disappeared in the river of yellow taxis and black cars weaving down Broadway.

The ZIA team took off their ZIA jackets and melted away into the crowd.

Mom K. and Dad K. stood looking at each other.

"So they are good guys?" said Dad K. "Bad guys?"

Mom K. folded her arms and looked off into the distance. "These guys are in their own world. And they are so beyond good guy/bad guy that we do not have the power to touch them . . . or even ask them anything."

"This is crazy," said Dad K.

"No," said Mom K. "This is big. Very big. And we are going to find out who they are and what they are up to."

"Yeah," said Dad K. "And so you are really a secret agent?"

"Yeah," said Mom K.. "And you are too?"

"Nice hat," said the old guy in the long black coat.

Dad K. remembered he was still wearing his aluminum foil. He snatched it off his head and stuffed it in his pocket.

"We have a lot to discuss," said Mom K., still staring off at the disappearing SUV. "But first I want something. I want . . . I want . . . I want Purple Nertz."

Symbiosis

The word "symbiosis" comes from two Greek words meaning "living" and "with." It is used to define the relationship between two organisms.

Some kinds of symbiosis are good for both organisms.

The oxpecker bird rides around on the backs of rhinos and eats harmful ticks off the rhino.

The rhino gets a healthy cleaning.

The oxpecker gets a good meal and nobody messing with him . . . or his rhino pal.

Chapter 22! MUCH WORSE

µ¨ç˙ ∑ø®ß´

Michael K. stormed down the crowded sidewalk, bumping into second graders and knocking over first graders without even seeing them.

His brain felt like it was on fire. It was hard enough to believe in aliens and saving the world in the first place. And now this? How much worse could it get?

The Spaceheadz had probably known about this from the beginning. They had just used him. He should have turned them in to the Anti-Alien Agency the first day he met them.

Michael K.'s elbow knocked a little girl's hat off her head.

"Hey!"

What was that guy's name? Agent Umber. He could have been a hero. And Michael K. could have been a hero too.

Michael K.'s backpack swung and shoved an old lady into a parking meter.

"Young man!"

Michael K. didn't care. He was done trying to save everyone.

"Michael K.! Michael K.!"

It was Bob and Jennifer and Venus and TJ running down the street to catch up with him. Michael K. did not want to be caught up with. He turned quickly and ducked into the Lots of Things toy store.

Michael K. tried to hide behind a wall of American Girl dolls and Barbies. But he couldn't even do that right. They found him.

"Michael K.," said Bob. "What is this wonderful place?"

"It has the **LOWEST PRICES OF THE SEASON!**" added Jennifer.

"Eeek week eeek eeek," said Major Fluffy.

"This must be Santa's North Pole. And you are going to ask the real Santa to help us?" asked Bob.

"No," said Michael K. "This is a toy store. And none of it is real. You only want all of the junk in here because ads have told you to want it." Michael K. grabbed a SpongeBob SquarePants off the shelf. "It's garbage. It's stupid. It's a scam just like Spaceheadz are a scam." Michael K. threw SpongeBob into a bin of Smurfs and Strawberry Shortcakes.

Bob and Jennifer stood shocked and speechless.

Venus grabbed Michael K.'s arm. "I don't think they knew about these bad Spaceheadz. They seem as surprised as we are."

"It is messed up," said TJ. "But Bob and Jennifer wouldn't do us like that."

Michael K. looked at the Spaceheadz. "Wouldn't they? We don't even know what they really look like on their planet. How can you know what they say is for real or not?"

"Eeek weee eeek eeek," said Major Fluffy. "Eeee eee eee eeek."

Venus typed Fluffy's squeaks into her Fluffy Speaks! app. She showed the translation to Michael K. and TJ.

```
WE ARE SPACEHEADZ GOOD.
WE NEED NEW, IMPROVED MICHAEL K.
```

Which is why no one saw the gray and white cat creep around the corner. The cat moved quickly and silently. She locked her green eyes on Major Fluffy. She twitched her tail once . . . twice . . . then jumped.

Bob bent down to inspect a Barbie Fairy-Tastic Princess. It was the only thing that saved Fluffy from the cat's outstretched claws.

The cat bounced off Bob's backpack, knocking Major Fluffy out and right into the Smurfs. The cat crouched for another pounce.

"Shoo!" said Venus.

"Don't mess with that hamster," said TJ.

"Oh, great," said Michael K.

The cat wasn't listening to anyone. She jumped again. Fluffy didn't wait for her to come down. He took off running down aisle three.

The cat jumped over the pile of plastic farm animals. She bounced off a bin of fairies and unicorns and took another swipe at Major Fluffy.

Fluffy zigged. Fluffy zagged. But the cat was too fast for him.

Fluffy jumped and climbed up the wall of stuffed animals and action figures. "Eeek eek meow meow," said Fluffy, pretending to reason with the cat.

But Fluffy was just stalling for time. He knew no one can reason with a cat.

The cat spit, "Mee oww wow," and went for the kill.

Fluffy dived between Iron Man and a brown and white ZhuZhu Pet.

Bob and Jennifer got to the shelf just in time to see the cat pounce, sink her teeth into a ball of fur, and run for the side door into the street.

"No!" yelled Bob. "Bad cat!"

But the cat was not listening. She was gone. And so was Major Fluffy.

"What are we going to do?" said Venus.

Michael K. didn't know what to do.

Was this for real? Or was this a big, fake setup too? And why did everybody have to keep coming to him to save the world . . . or save their hamster? . . .

BRAINWAVE

∫®åˆ˜∑å√´

"Ho, ho, ho," said the small man with the high-pitched voice and the Santa hat. "Wonderful party. Happy holidays to you all . . . and to all a good afternoon. Take the rest of the day off."

The man waved good-bye to the group of agents at the end of the hall.

The agents waved back.

"Thanks, Chief."

"Happy holidays."

"Have a good night."

The chief smiled and waved until the group had disappeared around the corner. Then he took off his Santa hat. His smile twisted into a sneer. He pressed the nose on the portrait of J. Edgar Hoover.

"Oh, you don't know what a good night I am planning to have. . . ."

The secret wall into the chief's office spun open.

The chief hurried through the dimly lit office. He sat at his desk, his pointy black AAA shoe tips just inches from Agent Umber's face.

He clicked on his wall monitor. A giant number filled the screen.

7

"So close!"

6

Umber squirmed under the desk. That voice sounded like the chief's. Maybe he should just pop out and say hello.

5

"Five."

But it was too late now.

4

"Four."

The chief was obviously busy.

3

"Three."

With some kind of very exciting counting project.

2

"Two."

It would probably be best to stay hidden.

1

"One."

And sneak out later.

"Spaceheadz! Yes! Yes! Yes! The earth's Brainwave is finally ours!" said the chief, spinning in circles around his office. "Ours! Ours! Ours!"

Umber peeked out from under the desk to see what was going on.

The hands on the chief's clock were spinning like crazy.

The chief's pencil sharpener whined like a tiny jet engine.

The pile of paper clips on the chief's desk whirled around in a micro tornado.

And then Agent Umber saw a sight his brain could not process. With every cheer and jump by the chief, the AEW monitor spiked into the red.

"YES!" said the chief.

AEW spike.

"OURS!" said the chief.

AEW spike.

The aliens had to be right here. Maybe they were invisible. Maybe the chief was in trouble.

Agent Umber pointed Hot Magenta's GUM recorder toward the center of the room. He would get all of this, capture the aliens, and save the chief.

The chief skipped to a file cabinet on the far wall. He unlocked the bottom drawer and pulled out a small glass globe. It looked like one of those snow globes you get with a little snowman in it. Except this globe didn't have anything in it. And on the base, instead of "Merry Xmas," it said: BRAINWAVE.

Umber pointed the GUM recorder at the scene in confused fear.

The chief twisted the globe into a port under the wall screen. He typed a quick command. The numbers on the Spaceheadz counter clicked quickly backward.

The globe glowed with a web of interconnected blue lines.

The chief laughed.

The AEW monitor spiked.

Umber's GUM recorder blinked its red recording light.

The Spaceheadz counter whizzed backward to zero and broke in half.

The chief unplugged the Brainwave globe, now completely filled with a network of crackling blue light. The chief stared into it like a hungry cat staring at a mouse.

Umber could not understand what he was seeing. But he was afraid. Something about that word the chief had yelled was very familiar. Spaceheadz. He had seen it somewhere before.

Umber decided he would record it all and show it to Agent Hot Magenta. She would know what it all meant.

The chief pocketed the globe and walked over to open his secret door. He stopped and looked around his office.

Umber held his breath.

The chief turned to push J. Edgar Hoover's

nose and . . . Umber's pocket started yodeling. More precisely—Umber's Picklephone® started yodeling.

Umber slapped at his phone. Umber poked at his phone. Umber strangled his phone and stopped it.

Too late.

Umber looked up to see the chief's face right in front of him.

"Agent Umber," said the chief. "What are you doing under my desk? Why are you dressed like a UUPS man?

"And why are you offering me a stick of gum?"

Agent Umber had no good answers for any of the chief's questions.

"I . . . uh . . . erh . . . ah . . ."

The chief pulled Umber out from under the desk. He sat Umber in the desk chair and gently took the GUM recorder out of his hand.

"I believe I have recorded some alien activity in your office and saved you, sir."

"Shhhhh," said the chief. He squeezed the GUM pack in one hand and instantly crushed it into a pile of wires and twisted metal.

"But that was the recording, Chief," said Umber.

"Agent Umber," said the chief. "You have been a great help to me. And you don't even—"

Umber's Picklephone® started yodeling again.

"Please make that stop," said the chief.

Umber pulled out his Picklephone® and slapped it.

The phone stopped yodeling and started blinking a red light. Umber put the Picklephone® in his shirt pocket.

"Got it, Chief. Now, let's track down those aliens."

The chief stared at Umber and shook his head. "Umber, Umber, Umber. As I was saying—you don't know what a great help you've been to me. So before I destroy you, I thought I should at least tell you what it is you've helped me with."

"I really did think those Little Red Riding Hoods could have been aliens, Chief. And those pizza guys? Still possible. And—"

"Agent Umber?"

"Yes, Chief?"

"I'm talking."

"Yes, Chief."

"And I am telling you that you don't have to worry about aliens anymore, because I AM THE ALIEN!"

The chief punched both fists into the air.

For a split second his entire human shape wavered in the air.

The AEW monitor spiked off the screen.

Agent Umber jumped from the chair, opened his mouth in speechless surprise, and backed away.

"Wha . . . wha . . . what?" stammered Umber.

The chief laughed a crazy evil-genius laugh just like crazy evil geniuses laugh in cartoons. He punched a button on his control board, and the wall screen lit up with a complete diagram of the chief's evil plan. He happily continued his explanation.

"Yes, I am an alien from the planet SPHDZ. I've been hiding in plain sight as the chief of this sorry AAA for years. I finally found three SPHDZ and their Earth-person friends who were smart enough to gather a three point one four million and one Brainwave for me. I have downloaded it into the Containment Globe. And now will use it to bllrrp planet Gonf!"

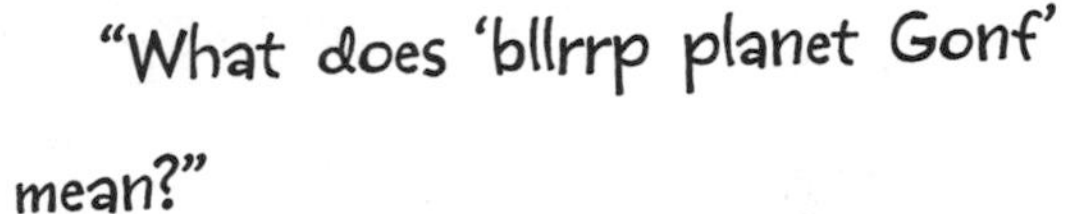

"What does 'bllrrp planet Gonf' mean?"

"It means the planet Gonf will be completely covered. Every living thing will be snuffed out. And Gonf will become the most perfect, the most beautiful, the most expensive-in-the-whole-universe . . . I forget your Earth-language name for it . . . oh, yes . . . parking lot!"

"No!" said Agent Umber.

"Yes," said the chief. "*That* has been the plan for the Brainwave all along. And I could not have done it without you helping by messing up every AEW investigation."

"No," said Umber, refusing to believe that the chief of the AAA could be an evil alien, refusing to believe his world had just been turned completely upside down, inside out, and frontside backward.

"Yes," said the chief. "And I could have done this so much sooner if your dad hadn't been such a problem. But I took care of him. And now there are only two small details that can stop me. One is that SPHDZ-helping kid. The other is you. Good-bye, Agent Umber."

"No, no, no," said Umber. He grabbed his head in both hands and stumbled backward.

The chief raised his AAA stapler and fired just as Umber bumped the portrait of J. Edgar Hoover right on the nose.

The secret wall spun open and Umber tumbled

out into the hall. The stapler/ray gun blast aimed at Umber's head missed, and exploded every can of soda inside the Coke machine instead.

Umber scrambled to his feet. He slipped on the Coke-covered floor. He grabbed the edge of a file cabinet and accidentally pulled it over, jamming the spinning secret wall and trapping the chief's arm.

"UMBER!" yelled the chief, or the evil Spaceheadz or whatever he was. "UMMMMMMBERRRRRRRR!!!" He fired blind stapler blasts up and down the hall.

The hands on the AAA clocks in the hallway spun wildly.

Umber jumped up from the puddle of Coke and ran.

He ran right, down the hall a bit, left, right, straight, right, left, left, right, another right, left, left, right, left, through a door, over a dropped meatball sub, and out a scuffed-up white door into a world that had completely changed for Agent Umber.

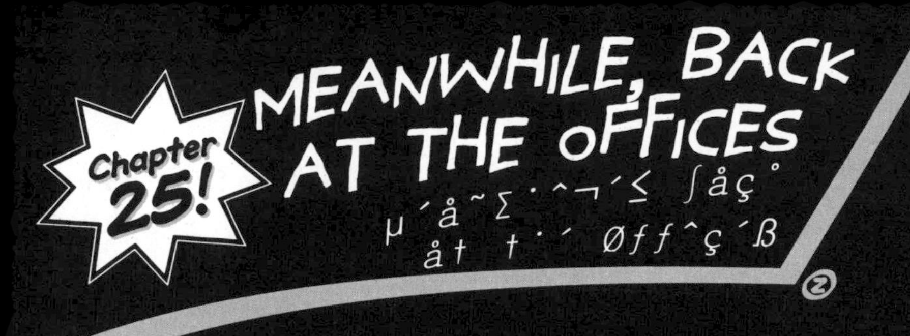

Dad K. dug through his Ad Factory papers and files for everything he had on DarkWave X.

There was nothing.

Every bit of it was gone.

Dad K. searched through his e-mail and computer files for anything with DarkWave X.

No results. Everything had been erased.

There was no proof that DarkWave X had ever existed.

Mom K. walked into Hair Today Styling Salon. She nodded to Chrissy. Chrissy nodded back.

Mom K. took her seat in the last chair.

Chrissy pressed the small green button on her spray nozzle.

The revolving wall spun Mom K. back into the secret ZIA offices.

Mom K. stood up. She had a plan. She was going to find out everything she could about this DarkWave X project.

She wanted to know who had okayed this, who was funding this, and exactly what this device was going to be used for.

But then Mom K. had a sudden and powerful urge.

Mom K. sat back down in the chair. She spun the wall back into the Hair Today Styling Salon.

Mom K. wanted to do something. She wanted to leave the office. She wanted to pick Baby K. up from Sunny Sun Sunshine Day Care. And she really, really wanted Purple Nertz.

Agent Umber collapsed in a sweaty and sticky Coca-Cola mess on Agent Hot Magenta's very cool couch.

He felt so shocked and drained and crazy that he didn't know whether to scream or cry or throw up.

He didn't do any of those things.

Umber sat, silent, while Hot Magenta questioned him. Again.

"So you got inside AAA HQ? You located the exact spot of the AEW spike? And that spot was the chief's office?"

Umber took off his UUPS hat and nodded.

Hot Magenta continued. "Then the chief came in? You hid? And you saw . . . ?"

Umber put his UUPS hat back on. He took it off again. He put it on.

Umber didn't want to say it again. It made no sense. And it destroyed everything he had always worked for.

"What did you see, Agent Umber?" said Agent Hot Magenta, folding her arms in front of her.

"Rrrrrrrrrr," growled Agent Wild Blue Yonder.

"I saw . . . I saw the chief," mumbled Agent Umber.

"And?"

Agent Wild Blue Yonder twitched her tail.

"The chief caught me. The chief told me . . ."

Umber couldn't say it.

"The chief told you . . . ?"

Twitch.

"The chief told me . . . the chief told me . . ."

It was almost too painful to even say. But once Umber started, everything came rushing out and there was no stopping.

"The chief told me he is really a Spaceheadz! An

alien! And he has been hiding in plain sight for years and years! And he made a plan to steal the Brainwave! And now he has it! And it was collected by three aliens and their human friends! And now the chief is going to use the Brainwave to bllrrp planet Gonf! Which is very bad! And the chief could do all of this only because I helped! I helped. I helped."

Umber pulled his UUPS hat down over his eyes and almost started crying.

"Meeee-OW," said Agent Wild Blue Yonder.

Agent Hot Magenta stared at Agent Umber. She tapped her upper lip with one finger.

"But you don't have any proof of this because . . . ?"

Agent Umber jumped up off the couch and acted out his description of what happened next. "Because the chief crushed the GUM recorder with one hand! And then he said he had to take care of that Spaceheadz kid and me and tried to blast my head off! But then I Leaping Lizard backflipped out of there, Thunder Hammer jammed his secret spinning wall with a file cabinet, and dodged the laser blasts from his stapler!"

Hot Magenta and Wild Blue Yonder gave each other a look.

"So the chief is really an alien who is planning to do something terrible and he shot at you with his stapler and you lost the recorder that would have shown all of this."

"Exactly!" said Umber. "We have to stop him! We have to protect and serve and always look up!"

Magenta sat down at her desk. Her antialienagency.com message alert chimed. While Umber paced back and forth talking plans, Magenta read the All Agents Alert. It was tagged ABSOLUTE TOP PRIORITY.

Immediate Action: Agent Umber has been wounded in an Alien Energy incident. He has lost his mind. He is very dangerous and has been relieved of all agent duties and privileges. All agents attempt capture. If you cannot capture Agent Umber, eliminate him. For the good of the entire planet.

Hot Magenta looked up at Umber walking around in circles, still talking to himself.

"Ah," said Agent Hot Magenta. "Now it all makes sense."

"Thank Goo-Goo Clusters you finally believe me," said Umber.

Agent Hot Magenta continued. "Overexposure to AEWs can cause all kinds of strange effects."

Umber froze in midstep. "What?"

Hot Magenta stood up and walked slowly toward Umber. "And I do remember reading somewhere that a weakness for alien delusions can be passed down from father to son."

"Mer-row," agreed Agent Wild Blue Yonder, circling behind Agent Umber.

"Alien delusions?" said Umber in a panicked voice. "Oh no! This is not a delusion. This is real. And we have to do something to stop the chief before it's too late."

Agent Hot Magenta put one hand on Umber's shoulder. "It's all over, Agent Umber. You were a good agent. We'll take care of the bad guys from here."

"The chief is an evil Spaceheadz," said Umber. "I saw it! He told me! If we don't stop him, he will use the Brainwave to bllrrp Gonf!"

Umber saw his career, his family history, his future, all ending in disgrace. He saw the planet Gonf getting bllrrped.

"Agent Umber, hand over your badge."

"No," whispered Umber. "No, no, no . . ."

Chapter 27! FLUFFY RIP

ƒ¬¨ƒƒ¥ ®ˆ∏

Michael K. stood staring at Bob and Jennifer staring at him, when he heard a familiar voice.

"Sweetie?"

A lady pushing a little kid in a stroller peeked around the shelves of Spider-Men, Supermen, and Wonder Women.

"Mom? What are you doing here?"

"I was going to ask you the same thing," said Mom K.

"Goo gah," said Baby K., holding both arms out for a hug.

Michael K. could never resist an invitation for a Baby K. hug. He hugged his sister.

"We are here because we need Michael K.," said Jennifer.

"Oh, hello, Jennifer," said Mom K. "That is very sweet."

"Yes," said Bob. "**WITH NO ARTIFICIAL FLAVORS!** Because a bad SPHDZ just took our Brainwave to use in an evil plan to bllrrp Gonf."

"That does sound terrible, Bob," said Mom K. She had no idea what he was talking about.

"And the **MEOW MEOW MEOW MEOW** just ate Major Fluffy," Bob added.

"Oh my . . . ," said Mom K. "And who is Major Fluffy?"

"Nobody," said Michael K., stepping in front of Bob and Jennifer to stop any more conversation.

Mom K. spotted Venus and TJ. "Hello, Venus and TJ. Michael, you should have told me you were here with all of your Spudz Club friends."

Michael K. shook his head. "Mom, for the millionth time, it's not Spudz. It's Spaceheadz. And they are not my friends. I was just—"

"—just telling us how important it is to help your friends," said Venus.

Michael K. frowned. That was not what he was going to say. At all.

"Michael K. can do anything," said Bob. "We need his **EXTRA CRUNCHY** help to find Fluffy and stop that bad SPHDZ."

That was it. The mention of the slogan from that stupid cereal commercial again pushed Michael K. over the edge. He couldn't take it anymore. He really and completely lost it.

"Ahhhhhyaaaayaaa!" yelled Michael K. "I cannot do everything! I'm just a kid. That was just a slogan from a commercial. I can't do anything!" Michael K. threw out both arms and knocked a pile of action figure packages off the shelf. "And you are going to have to face it, Fluffy is—"

"GOO!" said Baby K. She held up one of the action figure packages.

"Fluffy is—"

"Goo glar glar!" said Baby K. She smacked Michael K.'s leg with the package.

Michael K. took the bubble pack Baby K. was handing him. He held it up.

The action figure inside the clear plastic bubble said, "Eeek."

Michael K. blinked and looked again to be sure. The figure was not Iron Man. The figure was not Batman.

The superhero action figure was, somehow, Major Fluffy.

"Most exciting! One hundred percent fast-acting beat-down!" cheered Jennifer.

"Michael K. did it!" cheered Bob.

Venus and TJ cracked up laughing.

"Are you kidding me?" said Michael K. "I knew it! You just faked me out again to make me feel bad for you so I would help you. You knew he was okay the whole time!"

"What in the world is going on?" said Mom K.

Major Fluffy popped out of the bubble pack and, before anyone could stop him, started to explain everything.

"Eek eeek eee week—" explained Major Fluffy.

"Goo goo gah gah," said Baby K., interrupting.

"Gee blah goo blu?" asked Major Fluffy.

"Blah blu," answered Baby K., because she also knew much more about what was really going on with the chief, Agent Umber, the missing Brainwave, the ZIA, and DarkWave X.

Baby K. also had some very good thoughts on what to do about it.

"Goo. Gaah gaah blah blu blah blu. Buh buh buh. Ma ma ma ma blah goo gah gah. Gee geee geeeee. Nananana blah gah gaah gaaah. Blu blu. Gah gah goo gooo goooo geee blah blu."

Major Fluffy nodded.

Baby K. explained further.

"Blee gee blah goo gah. Gah gee blu bleee blah blah. Ber ber. Ner na na na new boo boo. Blah bah bah, pah ma ma, bee dah dah. Gaah gaah blah blu blah blu. Buh buh ba boo. Ma ma ma ma blah goo gah gah. Blee geee.

"Gaah gaah blah blu blah blu. Gluh buh buh. Ma blah goo gah gah. Gee geee. Gaah gaah blah blu blah blu blee buh buh. Glahma ma blah goo gah gah. Gee geee blah blu dah dah.

"Blah gah gaah gaaah. Blu blu. Gah gah goo pah ma ma, bee dah dah. Gaah gaah blah blu blah blu. Buh buh blah goo gah gah. Gee geee gaah gaah blah blu.

"Buh ma ma blah goo gah gah blah blu. Blah gah gaah gaaah. Blu blu. Gah gah goo pah ma ma, bee dah dah. Buh buh gla ma pah ma ma, bee dah dah. Gaah gaah blah blu blah blu. Buh buh buh. Ma gluh ma blah goo gah gah. Blee blu blah blu.

"Blu blah blu. Buh buh buh. Ma ma ma

ma blah goo gah gah. Gee geee geeeee. Nananana blah gah gaah gaaah. Blu blu. Gah gah goo gooo goooo geee blah blu.

"Blee gee blah goo gah. Gah gee blu bleee blah blah. Ber ber. Ner na na na new boo boo. Blah bah bah, pah ma ma, bee dah dah. Gaah gaah blah blu blah blu. Buh buh buh."

Major Fluffy could not believe that.

"Buh buh buh?" asked Major Fluffy.

Baby K. took a swig of her bottle and nodded yes. She elaborated.

"Gaah gaah blah blu blah blu. Buh buh buh. Ma blah goo gah gah. Gee geee blah blu. Dee dee dee.

"Blah gah gaah gaaah. Blu blu. Gah gah goo pah ma ma, bee dah dah. Gaah gaah blah blu blah blu. Buh buh buh. Gooo ma blah goo gah gah. Gee geee goo gaah gaah blah blu.

"Buh ma ma blah goo gah gah blah blu. Blah gah gaah gaaah. Blu blu. Gah gah goo pah ma ma, bee dah dah. Gaah gaah blah blu blah blu. Buh buh buh ma pah ma ma, bee dah dah. Gaah gaah dah blah blu blah blu. Buh buh buh. Ma gluh ma blah goo gah gah. Blee blu blah blu. Buh bee buh. Gee gee coo coo coo.

"Blu blu. Gah gah goo pah ma ma, bee dah dah. Gaah gaah blah blu. Gah gee blu bleee blah blah. Ber ber. Nuh na na na new boo boo. Blah bah bah, pah ma ma, bee dah dah. Gaah gaah blah blu blah blu. Buh buh gluh.

"Gaah gaah blah blu blah blu. Buh buh ma blah goo gah gah. Gee geee blah blu. Gah gah ger ger.

"Blah gah gaah gaaah. Blu blu. Gah gah goo pah ma ma, bee dah dah. Gaah gaah blah blu blah blu. Buh buh ma ma blah goo gah gah. Gee geee gaah gaah blah blu.

"Buh ma ma blah goo gah gah blah blu. Blah

gah gaah gaaah. Blu blu. Gah gah goo pah ma ma, bee dah dah. Gaah gaah blah blu blah blu. Buh buh ma pah ma ma, bee dah dah. Gaah gaah blah blu blah blu. Buh dee dee blah gooo."

Baby K. held up her empty bottle and smacked it into her open palm.

"Goo gah bla boo," said Baby K.

"Goo gah bla boo," Major Fluffy agreed.

Mom K. looked at Baby K.

Mom K. looked at Major Fluffy.

Venus pulled out her phone to log on to www.fluffysblog.com and use "Fluffy's Translator."

Michael K. looked at the Spaceheadz, Venus and TJ, his mom, and his baby sister. He had made up his mind. And he was sticking to it.

"Okay, Mom," said Michael K. "I have to get out of here. I'll see you at home."

Mom K. watched Michael K. walk out of the toy store and down the street. She looked down at Baby K. Baby K. smiled.

Mom K. shook her head like she was waking up from a nap.

Mom K. said, "Do you know if this store has Purple Nertz?"

Symbiosis II

In other symbiotic relationships one organism benefits and the other organism is not really helped.

Hermit crabs use old cast-off snail shells to protect themselves.

The remora (or suckerfish) attaches itself to sharks and whales and manta rays. The remora gets a free ride. The sharks and whales and manta rays get nothing.

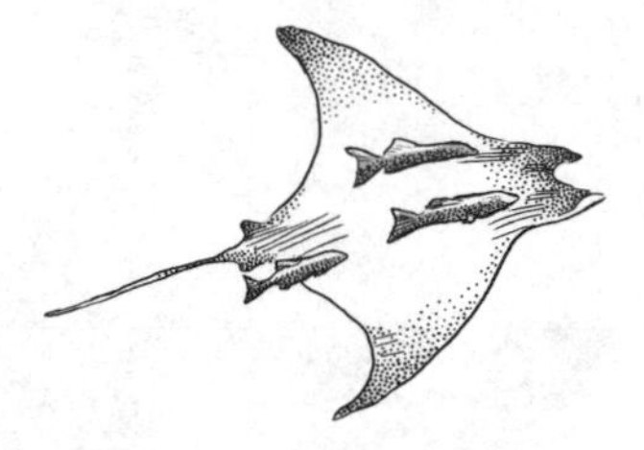

Your little sister always hangs around to get a lick of your ice cream cone.

Always.

NO

"No," mumbled Umber. "No."

"It's for your own good," said Agent Hot Magenta, speaking softly, and slowly slipping her right hand in over Umber's elbow for an Iron Arm Bar if he tried to run.

"You think the chief of the Anti-Alien Agency is an alien. You need help."

Agent Wild Blue Yonder crouched and gave another low, "Rowwwwrrr."

"The chief *is* an alien. A bad alien. A Spaceheadz. He told me himself."

Agent Hot Magenta guided Umber over toward the couch. She didn't want to hurt him when she flipped him over with a Flying Windmill. And she didn't want to break any of the equipment on her desk. "Agent Umber, we are AAA agents. You know it is our sworn duty to protect and to serve—"

"And to always look up," Umber finished.

"Exactly. If you had any real proof that this was true, Agent Wild Blue Yonder and I would fight side by side with you, protecting and serving. And looking up."

Agent Umber looked into Agent Hot Magenta's seriously blue eyes. "You would?"

"We would," said Agent Hot Magenta. "But you don't. So I am going to have to take you in. Give me your badge."

Agent Hot Magenta held one hand out to Umber . . . and slid the other behind his back to flip him.

Agent Umber suddenly felt very tired. He had tried so hard for so long to be a good agent. He really had. And now it didn't seem to matter. Well, at least he could make Agent Hot Magenta happy. She could be the one who brought Agent Umber in.

Agent Umber leaned sideways to pull his AAA badge out of his pocket. He lost his balance for a second. He stumbled. He hopped. He stepped in Wild Blue Yonder's water dish and flipped it, sending a sheet of water that completely drenched Agent Wild Blue Yonder.

The next part happened so fast that Agent Umber never saw it. But if he had been watching in slow motion, Umber would have seen

1. Wild Blue Yonder's eyes popping wide open

2. Wild Blue Yonder leaping straight up into the air in a twisting, hissing freak-out

3. Hot Magenta falling back in surprise

4. Hot Magenta flipping over the back of the couch and conking her head on the coffee table

5. Wild Blue Yonder landing on all fours and running to the corner to try to lick herself dry

Umber stood, his AAA badge in his outstretched hand, staring at the unconscious Agent Hot Magenta on her couch, and the soaking-wet Agent Wild Blue Yonder in the corner.

Umber checked Hot Magenta's pulse. She was fine. Just not conscious.

Umber looked at Wild Blue Yonder. She was not happy. She hissed.

Umber put a pillow under Hot Magenta's head. He flipped open his AAA badge and looked at it. He was still an AAA agent. He would still protect and serve.

But now it was time to run.

Agent Umber ran.

Chapter 31! ALWAYS LOOK UP

å¬∑å¥ß ¬øø˚ ¨π

The last of the weak winter sun slowly faded. It was night.

Cars and trucks and an occasional bus rolled over a round metal manhole cover with a *ca-clank*.

Down below this manhole cover, underground, under cover, Agent Umber arranged the few possessions he had managed to grab from his apartment before Agent Eggplant and Agent Jazzberry Jam almost caught him.

He should have known they would be watching his apartment. Too bad for them they didn't know the bathroom door always sticks. They weren't getting out of there for at least an hour.

But Umber would have to be more careful from now on. He was on the run, and a hunted man.

Agent Umber, dressed in four layers of AAA clothes, from AAA long underwear to an AAA winter poncho, shook out his AAA sleeping bag on a concrete ledge. He hung the picture of his mom and dad on a rusty nailhead. He placed his AAA toothbrush

ca-clank

in his AAA mug. He fluffed Agent Speedy's AAA towel

ca-clank

in his AAA gym bag to keep him warm.

Agent Speedy looked at Agent Umber and slowly blinked.

"This is how it's going to be," said Agent Umber. "Everyone is against us now. We'll hole up here tonight. Figure out our best moves

ca-clank

tomorrow."

Agent Speedy nodded.

Umber stretched out on his AAA sleeping bag. Up above, through one of the holes in the metal cover, Umber could just make out one bright evening star next to the thin crescent moon.

How could this be happening? All Umber ever wanted to do was be a good AAA agent. Now he was an AAA enemy. It was pretty sad that even Agent Hot Magenta thought he was the enemy. No one trusted him.

ca-clank

ca-clank

"And they will take everything away from me," Umber said to Speedy. "My AAA Cereal Box Laptop®, my AAA Battleship Decoder®, my AAA toothpicks . . ."

Umber felt through his AAA layers to pat his top shirt pocket. He pulled out a lumpy green object and held it up toward the evening star.

"But they won't take my AAA Picklephone®! And they can't stop me from sticking on this case until I get to the bottom of it!"

Agent Speedy closed his eyes and pulled his head into his shell.

"I will protect and serve and—"

"*BEEP,*" said the Picklephone®. "*You have one recording.*"

ca-clank

"*Beginning recording playback.*"

Umber looked at his Picklephone® in surprise. He heard his own voice saying, "*Got it, Chief. Now, let's track down those aliens.*"

Another voice answered, "*Umber, Umber, Umber. As I was saying—you don't know what a great help you've been to me. So before I destroy you, I thought I should at least tell you what it is you've helped me with.*"

It was the chief.

Agent Umber sat up in his AAA sleeping bag and cradled his Picklephone® in his hands. There was the shuffling of shirt pocket noise. More Umber talking. More

ca-clank

chief talking.

"Speedy, I think we've got it."

The recording continued. It was the chief. He was almost yelling, but he was perfectly clear. *"And I am telling you that you don't have to worry about aliens anymore, because I AM THE ALIEN!"*

Agent Umber listened through the whole recording. Twice. Then he called Agent Hot Magenta.

"Remember what you promised?"

"Umber! Where are you? I don't know how you escaped. But you have to turn yourself in."

"Remember you said you would fight side by side with me if I had proof about the chief?"

"Well, yes . . ."

"I have something you need to hear. Meet me under the North Star tomorrow morning at eight."

Agent Umber hung up his Picklephone® and lay back on his AAA sleeping bag.

ca-clank

So now he and Hot Magenta would stop the chief and foil his evil plan!

Wait. But how? The chief had this Brainwave thing, and no one knew what that might do. No one could stop the chief. . . .

ca-clank

No one except . . . what was that the chief said about "only two small details"?

Umber listened through his Picklephone® recording again.

ca-clank

". . . ALIEN! . . . Containment Globe . . . your dad . . . I took care of him . . . only two small details . . ."

There! Umber sat up in his sleeping bag, rewound, and played:

"And now there are only two small details that can stop me. One is that SPHDZ *-helping kid. The other is you. Good-bye, Agent Umber."*

"That's it, Speedy!" said Umber. "The kid with the other Spaceheadz must know what to do. They must be good Spaceheadz. Hot Magenta and I have to get to him before the chief does. And I know exactly where the good Spaceheadz live!"

Agent Speedy blinked and closed his eyes again.

Umber looked up and thanked his single twinkling lucky star.

ca-clank

Chapter 32! DELETE ALL

∂´¬´†´ å¬¬

After a stupid dinner—no one asked Michael K. anything about how his day went, or what was going on—Mom K. and Dad K. spent the rest of the night talking to each other and messing around with stuff in the dining room.

They didn't even come up once to check on him.

Michael K. closed his bedroom door, turned off his light, and lay on his back.

His phone buzzed with an incoming text.

Michael K. ignored it.

Another text.

Michael K. closed his eyes.

Another text.

And another.

Michael K. picked up his phone and read his texts.

VENUS
ARE YOU OKAY?
TELL ME WHAT U R THINKING.

TJ
WHAT'S UP?
HERE'S A SHOT OF OUR LATEST MISSION.

BOB
WE ARE IN DEEP-CLEANING TROUBLE.
HELP US, MICHAEL K.

JENNIFER
GET READY TO RUMBLE.
IT'S PAYBACK TIME.

MAJOR FLUFFY
EEEE EEK EEEK WEEK.
GOOO GLAR BOO BOO.

Michael K. put down his phone and rolled one of his finger skate-boards across his desk.

The Brainwave was gone. No doubt about that. That hurt. He had been suckered into helping put the whole scam together. That hurt even worse.

Michael K. ollied up onto his science book.

So now what? If the Space-headz and General Accounting were telling the truth—and that was still a big if—this planet Gonf was going to get bllrrped. But how bad would that be?

Nosegrind along the desk edge.

Okay, pretty bad for everything that lived on planet Gonf. But it's not like he knew anybody on Gonf. And maybe they were just a bunch of creepy-looking slugs or something that lived on Gonf. So who would care?

Kickflip over the pencil.

That would be pretty bad to have everything on your whole planet killed just to have it turned into a parking lot. Especially if somebody could stop it.

Frontside boneless to helicopter.

Yeah, but maybe it was also just another big fake. And then when someone saved the planet Gonf, it would turn out that there was another planet in worse trouble that someone would have to save.

Vert to spacewalk.

Tomorrow was a new day. He had a plan, and he would stick to it.

Michael K. picked up his phone, hit the edit button, then

DELETE ALL

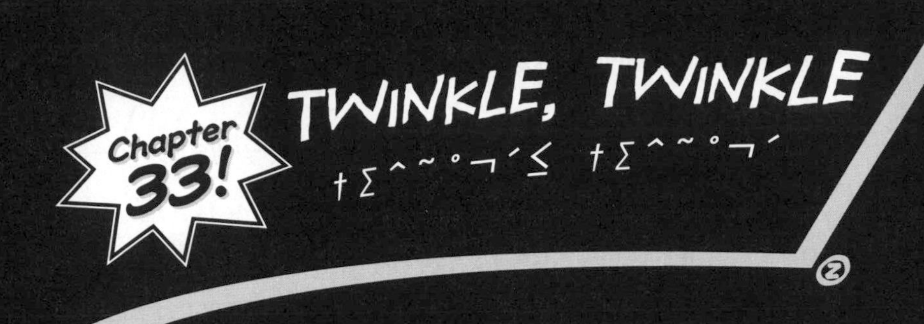

Eight o'clock.

Directly under the North Star.

A puffy-shaped man in a blue poncho carrying a rolled-up sleeping bag and a gym bag approached a woman with hot pink shoes.

The man pulled a pickle out of his pocket and handed it to her.

The woman listened to the pickle.

She put one hand on her forehead and listened again.

The woman handed the pickle back to the man. She picked up his gym bag. They walked out past Orion, Cassiopeia, and the Big Dipper.

PLANETARIUM
EXIT

The man and the woman got into the woman's very cool-looking carbon black BMW M6 and roared off to fight side by side.

A small woman in a sea blue outfit and strands of multi-colored beads sat in an illegally parked van outside the planetarium. The sign on the van read: AAA SEA MONKEY WRANGLERS.

The woman watched the BMW disappear down the street.

She took out a phone shaped like a starfish and texted an All Agents Alert. Two seconds later the text was sent to every NYC-area AAA agent.

Every AAA agent except Agent Hot Magenta and Agent Umber.

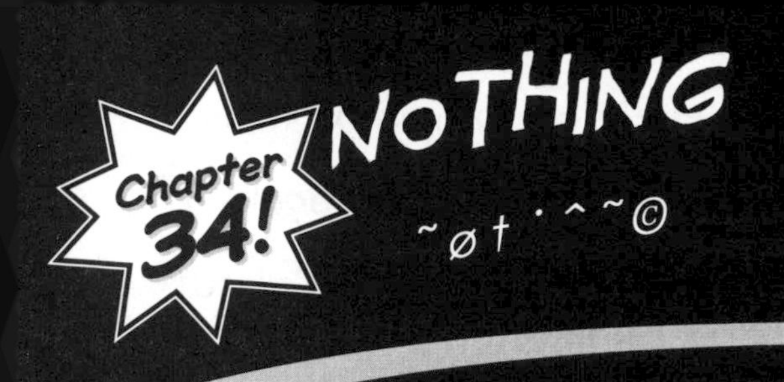

Michael K. walked into morning homeroom. Venus and TJ were already in their usual seats in the back of the room. Bob and Jennifer sat next to them. Fluffy sat quietly in his cage.

Michael K. sat down in the very front row, next to Lisa, in a seat he never sat in.

"Hello," said Michael K. "I'm Michael K."

Lisa took Michael K.'s hand and shook it because she didn't know what else to do.

"Yeah, I know," said Lisa. "We've been in class for, like, half a year already."

"I'm starting over again," said Michael K.

"You're starting fifth grade all over again?" said Lisa. "In the middle of the year? Can you do that?"

Michael K. did that.

He stayed in the front row and raised his hand to answer every question about the reading book, *The Tale of Despereaux*, even though it was a book about a mouse who loves a princess.

He sat at the table with Jackson, Madison, Raoul, and two kids whose names he didn't even know for the whole holiday party.

He pretended he didn't even see Bob and Jennifer.

He pretended to laugh when Joey told a bad knock knock joke about an elf.

When Venus and TJ came to his table and Venus said, "Michael K., what are you doing?" Michael K. answered, "Nothing."

"Michael K., you are an idiot," said Venus. "And you are a terrible friend."

Michael K. kept doing nothing until the party was over, the half school day was done, and everyone walked out the door of 501-B for winter vacation.

Bob and Jennifer left with Venus and TJ.

Michael K. felt relieved. Then he felt terrible.

Having no friends was turning out to be worse than having weird friends.

Michael K. bit the head off a Frosty the Snowman and threw the body back on the tray of holiday fruitcake, elf cupcakes, and reindeer gumdrops.

This is crazy," said Dad K.

"We went over everything last night," said Mom K. "It's the only way. We don't know who we can trust."

Dad K., dressed in white overalls to look like a sign painter/billboard installer, lowered Mom K. on the climbing rope from the top of the giant underwear ad.

The morning traffic in Times Square down below looked like a swarming colony of ants.

Mom K. swung back and forth, right next to a huge belly button.

"IS THAT IT?" Dad K. called down.

Mom K. felt around for a latch or handle. "The blueprint showed it is right around here somewhere."

Dad K. watched an NYC police van drive down Seventh Avenue. A light changed red and a small mob of people flowed across the street. No one looked up.

Dad K. checked the rope looped around a pipe, and reviewed their plan:

1. Approach IWANT Pulsar from above to avoid guards below.
2. Remove memory pod from IWANT Pulsar.
3. Get it to the president right away.
4. Do not leak any info to Mom K.'s ZIA or Dad K.'s DarkWave X.

"Got it!" said Mom K.

She popped open a hidden hatch panel and swung herself through the underwear model's belly button.

JEANS
CAN YOU

Dad K. let out some slack.

Forty-six seconds later Mom K. tugged on the rope to signal she was ready to be pulled up.

"Amazing," said Dad K. He wondered what else Mom K. knew how to do.

Dad K. pulled. Mom K. scrambled up the mostly naked lady. She handed Dad K. the black memory pod and crawled over the top of the sign.

"You did it," said Dad K.

The two fake billboard installers sat down behind the giant ad.

"This will stop anyone from using this thing," said Mom K. "And give us the proof we need to stop this operation. It's too dangerous. I still kind of feel like I want Purple Nertz."

Dad K. smiled.

Mom K. slid a latch and opened the memory pod.

Something was not right. There was supposed to be a row of computer chips slotted into this pod. Instead there was only a small piece of paper.

Mom K. took out the piece of paper. She unfolded it, read it, and handed it to Dad K.

Dad K. read it. Dad K. dropped it.

"This could be trouble," said Mom K.

Mom K. and Dad K. looked all around, then headed for the emergency exit.

Chapter 36! ANGELS SINGING

å˜©´¬ß ß^˜©^˜©

Agent Umber, wearing a curly gray wig, big brown-rimmed glasses, a pretty blue-flower-patterned dress, a light green overcoat, and a sensible purse and shoes, stepped slowly down the back stairs.

Agent Hot Magenta, in a man's charcoal gray suit and tie, long black winter coat, and black wing tips, with her hair tucked under a black fedora, pressed her mustache against her top lip and followed sweet-old-lady Agent Umber.

"I still think we should have used my idea for disguises," said Umber.

"The idea is to not draw attention to ourselves," said Agent Hot Magenta. "And I don't think we would do that as Princess Leia and Chewbacca. Every AAA agent in the world is looking for you."

"I could have been a stormtrooper," said Agent Umber. He slammed open the door to the back alley like a stormtrooper.

The door smacked a man who had been standing on the other side, knocking him right into a trash can.

"Oops, sorry, dearie," said Agent Umber in his best old-lady voice.

Hot Magenta went to help the man out of the garbage can, then noticed he was dressed as a cat burglar. She used the lid to slam him deeper into the can and hustled Agent Umber out to the sidewalk.

"Good shot. That was Agent Black."

Umber and Hot Magenta blended into the morning-rush-hour crowd of people headed for the subway.

"We have to be ready for anything," said the mustached man to the sweet old lady.

"Right," said the sweet old lady. "I knew that."

A newspaper guy at the entrance to the subway handed the sweet old lady a paper . . . then made a grab for his wrist.

Mustached Magenta sidestepped in, grabbed the guy's pinkie finger in a pressure point hold, walked him over to his van, and threw him into the back without anyone noticing. She jammed a broomstick through the door handles, locking him inside.

"Agent Radical Red," said mustached Magenta.

"Oh, look," said sweet-old-lady Umber, reading the free paper, "the Christmas sale on tree decorations starts today."

Hot Magenta guided Umber down to the subway platform, scanning everyone and everything.

The subway train pulled into the station. The doors opened, and what looked like a small boy ran out straight for Umber.

Old-lady Umber, still reading the paper, turned to mustached Magenta. "And all Christmas lights are fifty percent off!" As Umber turned, his purse spun and whacked the boy in the eye. The kid went down in a heap.

Hot Magenta hustled Umber onto the subway. The doors closed, and she got a closer look at the "boy."

"Agent Wild Watermelon."

"What?" said Umber.

"We have to find these good Spaceheadz and this kid before anyone else does," said Hot Magenta. "Are you sure you know where they are?"

A polite gentleman stood to give old-lady Umber his seat. Umber sat down. The train stopped at the next station. The polite gentleman tried to slip a pair of handcuffs on Umber. Hot Magenta spun him around, slapped his own handcuffs on him, and shoved him out the door onto the platform.

"Magic Mint."

"I'm pretty sure I know," said Umber, using his old-lady voice, and starting to like it. "I saw their stickers when the chief first put me on the case. I saw their signs down on the avenue. I almost had them at that school play. It has to be them. And the chief said it himself. Me and the kid are the only two details who can stop his evil plan."

The subway screeched to a stop at their station.

The doors opened. Hot Magenta karate-chopped a large guy in plumber's coveralls back into his seat. Umber stomped a Chinese lady's foot with an accidental heel that left her hopping as the doors closed.

"I sure hope you're right," said Hot Magenta. "Mountain Meadow and Jungle Green."

Umber and Hot Magenta left the subway station

without incident. But on the short walk from the subway to Fifth Avenue, Umber and Hot Magenta

1. dodged Agent Almond dropping from a tree

2. crashed Agent Purple Pizzazz, trying to mow them down with a bus

3. wrapped Agent Mauvelous in her own swinging tinsel shot

4. dropped Agent Piggy Pink into his tiger trap

5. and completely tangled the net drop/shaving cream/stink bomb attack of Agents Copper, Violet, and Neon Carrot

Agent Hot Magenta and Agent Umber stood in front of a wooden door, just down the street from a neon sign blinking JACKIE'S 5TH AMENDMENT, covered with stickers that read SPHDZ . . . **BE** SPHDZ . . . SPHDZ **= GOOD**.

"Agent Umber," said Agent Hot Magenta, fixing her mustache. "I didn't think you had it in you. But you are a real AAA agent."

Agent Hot Magenta knocked on the Spaceheadz' door.

Little-old-lady Umber smiled and felt the best he had ever felt. He saw hearts and rainbows. He heard Agent Hot Magenta talking to a girl who answered the door. He thought he heard angels singing. . . .

The angels singing turned out to be the little girl in the Spaceheadz' doorway screaming, "AAA agents! Run! Run for your lives!"

Michael K. sat at his desk in his room.

Mom K. and Dad K. were off somewhere doing who knows what. Baby K. was at her Sunshine Whatever Baby Place.

The whole house was terribly quiet.

Michael K. stared at his computer screen.

"Three point one four million and nothing," said Michael K. to no one in particular.

Michael K. closed the browser window, clicked on his spaceheadz.com bookmark, and dragged it into his computer screen trash.

"Three point one four million and . . . one big sucker," said Michael K. to the whole world.

Michael K. shut down his computer.

He pulled his SPHDZ certificate down from his bulletin board and threw it in the trash.

He ripped his SPHDZ sticker off his skateboard and threw it in the trash.

He tore down his SPHDZ posters and threw them in the trash.

He ran around his room pulling, yanking, tearing, and trashing anything and everything SPHDZ.

Michael K. sat down on his bed.

The house was still terribly quiet.

"I don't need them," said Michael K. "I do not need them."

And then he picked up his science book to try to read and forget about everything.

Symbiosis III

And in the most lopsided symbiotic relationship one organism benefits and the other organism is harmed.

Ticks suck blood from larger animals, leaving the animals with nothing but disease and ugly red spots.

The parasitic wasp injects eggs inside a living caterpillar. The eggs hatch and eat the caterpillar from the inside out.

You do all of the work for the big history project. Somebody else takes all of the credit and says you didn't help.

The organism doing the freeloading and harming is called a parasite.

AFTER THESE MESSAGES

åft´® †˙´ß´ µ´ßßå©´ß

Bob and Jennifer and Fluffy sat soaking up the energy from three simultaneous car commercials.

"... feel the difference ..."

"... power to spare ..."

"... like never before ..."

Bob fiddled with the hair on his yellow Magic Star pony.

Jennifer chewed a giant I VISITED FLORIDA pencil.

Fluffy rocked back and forth like a sad, crazy bear in an old zoo.

"This is awful," said Venus.

"Mad crazy," said TJ.

"Some side effects may occur," said Bob.

"Not ***LIKE A GOOD NEIGHBOR***," said Jennifer.

Jennifer entered the code BLLRRP GONF into imsuregladthatdidnthappen.com again to show General Accounting's latest transmission.

Venus and TJ watched the terrible truth. Again.

TJ could still not believe it. "So General Accounting and his other bad Spaceheadz pal are going to use our Brainwave . . . that we worked our butts off to collect . . . to turn a whole planet into . . . a parking lot?"

"One hundred percent," said Jennifer, finishing the last of her souvenir pencil. "Just as General Accounting shows us."

"No. Way," said Venus. "How do we stop this?"

Bob and Jennifer and Fluffy looked blank.

There was a knock on the door.

"Now what?" said Venus. She went to the front door and looked out the peephole. "It's a funny-looking old lady with big glasses and a guy in a suit with a bad mustache. Are they friends of yours?"

Venus opened the door. The funny old lady just stood there, spacing out with a dreamy look on her face.

"Can I help you?"

"I hope so," said the man with the bad mustache. He flipped open a badge holder. "We are with the AAA. And we need to speak to Spaceheadz."

Venus screamed, then yelled, "AAA agents! Run! Run for your lives!"

But the agents pushed their way in and closed the door behind them.

There was no way out.

This was it. The Spaceheadz were ultimately, and finally, trapped.

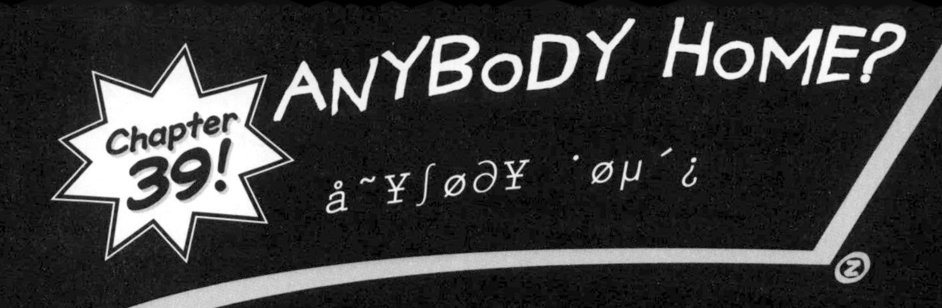

Dad K. slid his Ad Factory ID, made to look like an old-fashioned time card that you slid into an old-fashioned punch clock, into the buzzer at the Ad Factory main entrance.

Nothing happened.

Dad K. wiped the ID on his billboard installer overalls and tried again.

Still nothing.

Dad K. banged on the fake garage door.

Nobody answered.

It was awfully dark in there for the middle of the day.

Dad K. banged again.

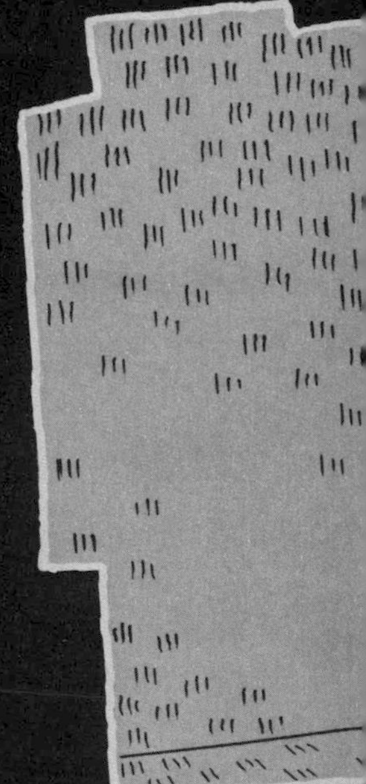

"Maybe everyone is at the company holiday party," said Mom K.

"Yeah, maybe," said Dad K. "But I think that's tomorrow. And Mechanic Joe, our receptionist, is always at the front desk. But it looks like the lobby is empty."

"That's weird," said Mom K., getting a little nervous. "Let's go over to my office and use the ZIA computers."

Mom K. and Dad K. picked up their ropes and headed for the Hair Today Styling Salon.

". . . and that is how this guy, who has always been the chief of the AAA, took your Brainwave. I saw the whole thing," said the sweet old lady, who was now a man with a curly gray wig and glasses in his lap.

"It's true," said the man, who was now a woman with long blond hair and a mustache and a hat in her lap. "We have the proof."

Venus felt her head spinning. But that might have been from all of the running around and yelling that she had done before the AAA agents caught her, calmed her down, and explained that they weren't going to turn the Spaceheadz in . . . because they were trying to stop a bad Spaceheadz . . . and they needed their help as good Spaceheadz????

"Eeeek eee eee eeek," said Major Fluffy.

Bob and Jennifer didn't say anything. They were still completely scared to be this close to AAA agents. They just nodded.

"Whoa," said TJ, putting it all together. "So this boss of your whole Anti-Alien outfit turns out to be an alien himself?"

"Exactly," said Agent Hot Magenta.

TJ smacked his fist in his palm. "So he must be the other bad Spaceheadz who is General Accounting's pal."

"And he must be the one who stole the Brainwave to bllrrp Gonf!" added Venus.

"I have no idea what that means," said Agent Hot Magenta. "But it doesn't sound good."

"But what can we do to help?" asked Venus.

Agent Hot Magenta played with her mustache. "The chief let it slip that he can only be stopped by Agent Umber . . . and 'that Spaceheadz-helping kid.'" Agent Hot Magenta turned to Venus. "We believe that kid is the key to stopping this whole mess. And we believe that kid is you."

"Oh, no," said Venus.

"Or maybe you?" said Umber, looking at TJ.

"I don't think so," said TJ.

"Squeee eek eek eek," said Major Fluffy.

Bob and Jennifer nodded.

"Did that hamster say something?" said Agent Umber.

"Yes," said Bob. "There is only one Earth-person kid who can stop bad SPHDZ."

Venus and TJ said his name at exactly the same time: "Michael K."

Agent Hot Magenta looked around. "So where is this Michael K.?"

"He's probably over at his house," said Venus.

"Oh no," said Agent Umber. "We might be too late."

"We have to go now," said Agent Hot Magenta. "And hope we get to him before the other guys do."

ANYBODY HOME?

å˜¥∫ø∂¥ ˙øµ´¿

Mom K. went to push open the glass door to the Hair Today Styling Salon . . . and almost bounced her head off the glass.

The door was locked.

The door was never locked in the middle of the day.

Either Carol or Chrissy was always at her station.

Mom K. put her hand against the glass and looked in.

The room was completely empty, except for a single push broom over in one corner. No chairs. No sinks. No dryers. No mirrors. No tables. No magazines.

No Carol.

No Chrissy.

Mom K. stepped back from the door to double-check and be sure she was at the right address.

No sign.

You could just barely see a faint outline of where the letters HAIR TODAY had been on the building.

"Not good," said Mom K.

"So not good," said Dad K.

And in the next second they had the exact same thought.

They flagged down a cab.

Dad K. said, "Sunny Sun Sunshine Day Care!"

Mom K. added, "As fast as you can."

Chapter 42! KNOCK, KNOCK

°˜øç°≤ °˜øç°

Venus was the first to reach Michael K.'s door. She felt terrible that she had said those mean things to Michael K. And that those things might be the last words he ever heard from her.

Venus banged on Michael K.'s door.

"Michael K., open up. It's me."

Nobody answered.

TJ, Bob, Jennifer, Fluffy, Umber, and Hot Magenta raced up the front stairs.

Bob and Jennifer banged on the door.

"**GRAB LIFE BY THE HORNS**, Michael K.!"

Nobody answered.

"What will they do to him?" said Venus.

Agent Hot Magenta shook her head.

"Nothing good," said Agent Umber. "They will want to eliminate him."

Hot Magenta saw the panicked look on Venus's face and elbowed Umber to get him to shut up.

"Ouch," said Umber. "Watch where—"

"Oh, Michael K.," said Venus.

The door suddenly opened. And there, holding the doorknob, was . . .

"Michael K.!" said Bob.

"Wha? . . . Who? . . . Whoa!" said Michael K. when he saw Agent Umber. He stepped back into the hallway and half closed the door.

Bob, Jennifer, Venus, TJ, and Fluffy poured into Michael K.'s house and pushed Michael K. into the living room, every-

one talking at once. Agents Umber and Hot Magenta closed the door, double locked it behind them, and followed.

"... bad Spaceheadz ..."

"... thought you were snatched ..."

"... destroy a whole planet ..."

"... parking lot! ..."

"... only one SPHDZ kid can stop ..."

"... **EXTRA CRUNCHY** ..."

"... AAA agents helping us ..."

"... eeee eeek eeek ..."

Michael K. sat on the edge of Dad K.'s big living-room chair. He could hardly believe they were here. The Spaceheadz and the AAA. In the same room.

". . . so we really need you, Michael K.," said Venus.

"The whole world needs you," said Agent Umber, pulling up his flowered dress.

"Quite possibly the whole galaxy needs you," said Agent Hot Magenta.

Michael K. was flattered to think that the whole galaxy might need him. And it was pretty nice of TJ and Venus to be worried about him.

But that was just . . . just . . . stupid. How did he know this wasn't just some big AAA setup? Why were they suddenly so interested in helping aliens? The name of their organization was the ANTI-Alien Agency.

He did not want to be a sucker again.

"I don't know," said Michael K. "I don't . . ."

Everyone heard the front door open.

Agents Umber and Hot Magenta jumped to

their feet and crouched in a Karate Kill pose on either side of the living-room doorway.

Someone was sneaking in the front hall.

Bob covered his eyes.

A three-headed black shadow fell across the doorway.

"Oh, hi, Mom. Hi, Dad. Hey, Baby," said Michael K.

Mom K. and Dad K. froze in midstep.

Umber and Hot Magenta dropped their Kill pose and pretended they were just looking at the wallpaper.

"What are you guys doing wearing white coveralls?" asked Michael K. "And what's with the climbing rope?"

"Oh, nothing, sweetie," said Mom K. "Your dad and I were

just . . . um . . . working on . . . um . . . a project of ours."

"Goo gar goo," said Baby K.

"Eeek squee eek," answered Fluffy.

Mom K. and Dad K. looked more closely at the crowd in the living room. They saw the Spaceheadz, Venus and TJ, a man in a suit with very long hair, and a rather funny-looking woman in a crooked wig.

"Who are your new friends?" said Mom K.

"And what is the Spudz Club up to?" said Dad K.

"Oh, nothing," said Michael K. "We were just talking about stuff."

Everyone stood and sat around very awkwardly, everyone pretending they were something or someone they were not, everyone pretending they were not doing something they really were.

There is no telling how long this uncomfortable shuffle would have gone on, because exactly twelve seconds after it started, it ended when an attack team of men and women dressed in elf costumes and reindeer horns and led by a Santa crashed in every door and window in the K. family house.

GOAT RODEO

©øåt ®øð´ø

Everybody over on the couch," said the Santa with the mirrored sunglasses and the sleeves ripped off his red velvet jacket.

Santa held a very large power-charge blaster that looked like it could shock everyone into next week.

Agent Hot Magenta calculated how she could take out Santa, chop-block the lead elf, and sweep-kick two of the reindeer.

That still left another Santa, two armed elves, and three killer reindeer.

Not good.

Too many innocent civilians in the line of fire.

Michael K. tried to figure out if he could lead everyone in a mad charge out.

No way.

Mom K., Dad K., Michael K., Baby K., Venus, TJ, Jennifer, Bob, Fluffy, Hot Magenta, and Umber shuffled over toward the couch.

"Uh, I don't think we can all fit on the couch," said Michael K.

"Okay," said Santa. "Some people sit on the couch. Some people sit in chairs. The rest of you people sit on the floor."

"Santa Claus, we are so glad to see you!" said Bob.

"Sit!" said Santa.

Bob sat.

Everyone else sat. This looked like the end. The end of everything.

Santa took off his shades.

"Delta?" said Dad K.

"Hey there, ad guy," answered Santa.

"Echo?" said Mom K.

One of the elves gave a little wave.

"Foxtrot?"

The reindeer by the front window nodded.

"Listen," said Dad K. "We didn't do anything to the IWANT Pulsar. It was empty when we got to it. And these kids and the nice older lady and the gentleman with long blond hair don't have anything to do with this."

"Shut your piehole, ad guy," said Santa. "Everybody in this room has everything to do with this. The global situation has gone seriously sideways. We are in a Code Red Plus here, people. We need total cooperation. And we need it now. Understood?"

"I won't let you take the kid," said Agent Umber. "I know twelve different fighting styles."

"Zip it, lady," said Santa. He checked his big army-green watch. "Sixteen hundred. Foxtrot. Run 'em down, fill 'em in, and then let's do this."

The lady reindeer stood in front of the couch. She pulled a shiny metal pointer out of somewhere and quickly pointed around the room.

"Bob, Jennifer, Major Fluffy—Spaceheadz from the planet Spaceheadz. Also sometimes abbreviated as SPHDZ.

"Venus, TJ—human. But accomplices in gathering the three point one four million and one Spaceheadz Brainwave.

"Mom K.—ZIA operative.

"Dad K.—ad guy and DarkWave X egghead.

"Baby K.—baby.

"Agent Hot Magenta, Agent Umber—AAA agents. Also on the run."

If there were a sound made by dropping jaws, there would have been a sonic boom.

DarkWave X knew exactly who everyone was. And they knew exactly what everyone was doing.

Before anyone could ask anything—and there was a lot that everyone wanted to ask—Delta Santa took over the pointer.

"And here's the situation, people. The bad guys have stolen this very powerful Brainwave. They are planning to do very bad things with it. That cannot happen."

Delta Santa smacked his palm with the pointer.

"We have developed a WantWave capable

of holding off the Brainwave. But not for long. We need something bigger. Something more. And our intel tells us we need all of you . . . and one more very important piece."

Santa pointed the metal rod at one person.

"You, kid. Michael K.—Spaceheadz leader."

Everyone in the room looked at Michael K.

In his darkened office the chief hunched over the small glass globe filled with the crackling blue web.

He read the message from his fellow plotter:

∫®å^˜∑å√´ ˆß ø¨®ß. ˜ø
∑å√´ƒø®µ çå˜ ß†øϖ ¨ß ˜ø∑.

He sent a return message:

ø¨®ß ø¨®ß ø¨®ß. †∑ø ßµå¬¬
∂´†å^¬ß †ø ƒ^˜^ß øƒƒ.
†·˜ ©ø˜ƒ ˆß ∫¬¬®®ϖ.

HOO RAH

˙øø ®å˙

Delta Santa locked Michael K. in his steely gaze. He gave his palm another sharp whack with the pointer.

"That's the straight story. But last time I checked, this is still a free country. So it's your choice, soldier. You in? You out?"

"So you are not the bad guys?" asked Dad K.

"We are not the bad guys," Delta Santa answered. He checked his watch again and looked to Michael K. for his answer.

"The time right now is just-about-too-late o'clock. You've got one shot at this, kid. And then you are with us, or you never heard of us. What'll it be?"

A cold wind blew in the broken doors and windows.

Michael K. looked at Bob and Jennifer. Were they in on this?

Michael K. looked at his mom and dad. How come they hadn't told him what they were really doing?

Michael K. looked at Agents Umber and Hot Magenta. Umber's old-lady disguise was the worst disguise he had ever seen.

Michael K. looked at TJ and Venus. They really were good friends. So maybe it would be best if he didn't drag them any deeper into this mess.

Everyone, and Santa and his elves and reindeer, waited to hear Michael K.'s answer.

"I don't know what I am supposed to know or what I'm supposed to be doing," said Michael K.

Delta Santa twisted his lip to one side and gave a look to his team to get ready to take off.

Umber looked like he was going to cry.

Venus squeezed her hands together.

Michael K. stood up. "But we started this Spaceheadz mission together. Let's finish this mission Spaceheadz-style together. I say yes."

The Spaceheadz, the humans, the Santa, elves, and reindeer cheered.

"Eeek ee squee eee," said Fluffy.

"Goo glah goo goo," said Baby K.

Venus smiled at Michael K. Michael K. smiled at Venus.

Michael K. had no idea what he was

getting into. And he didn't know if he was being brave, or being the biggest idiot in the whole galaxy.

But he did know he was with real friends.

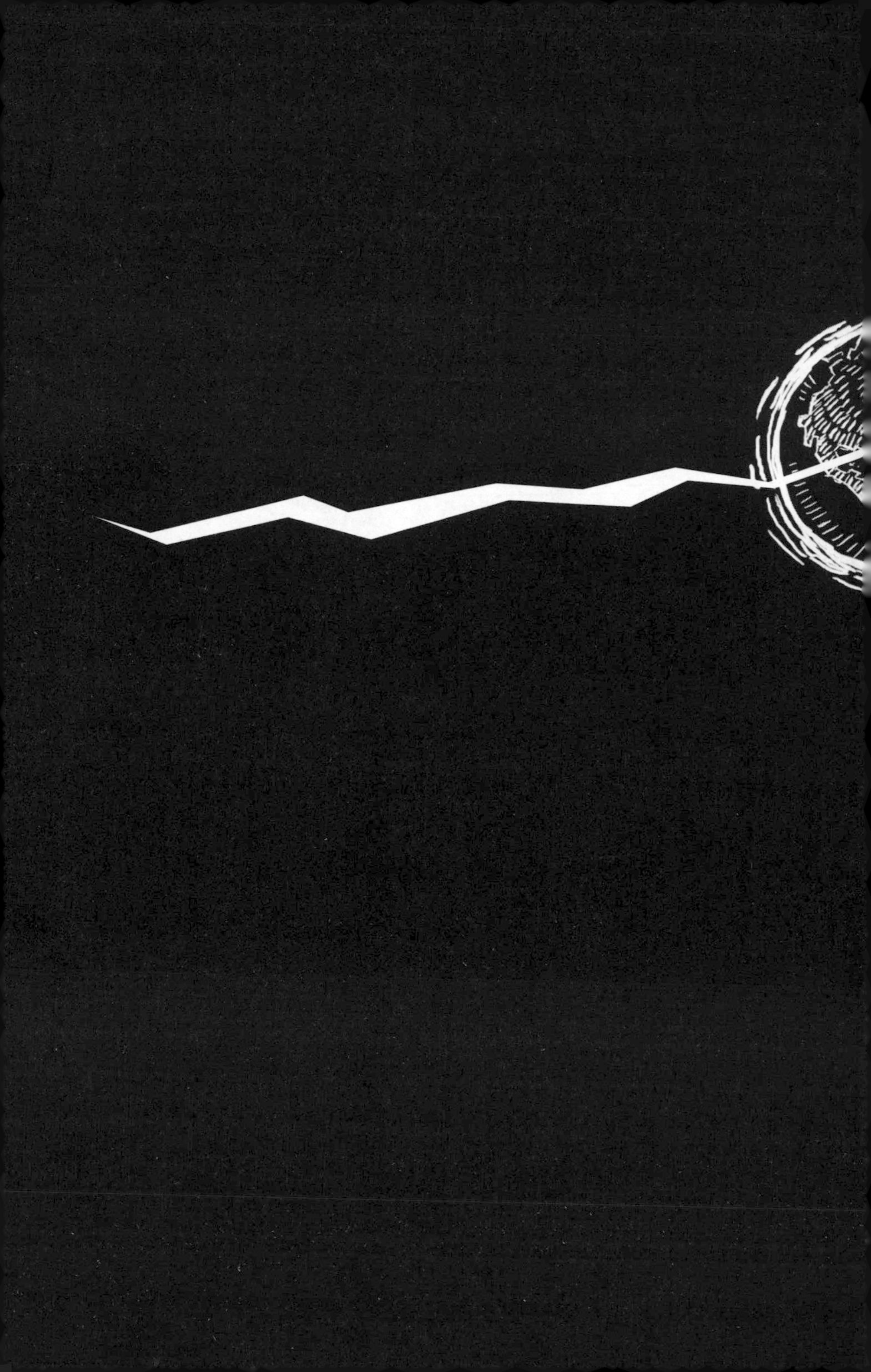

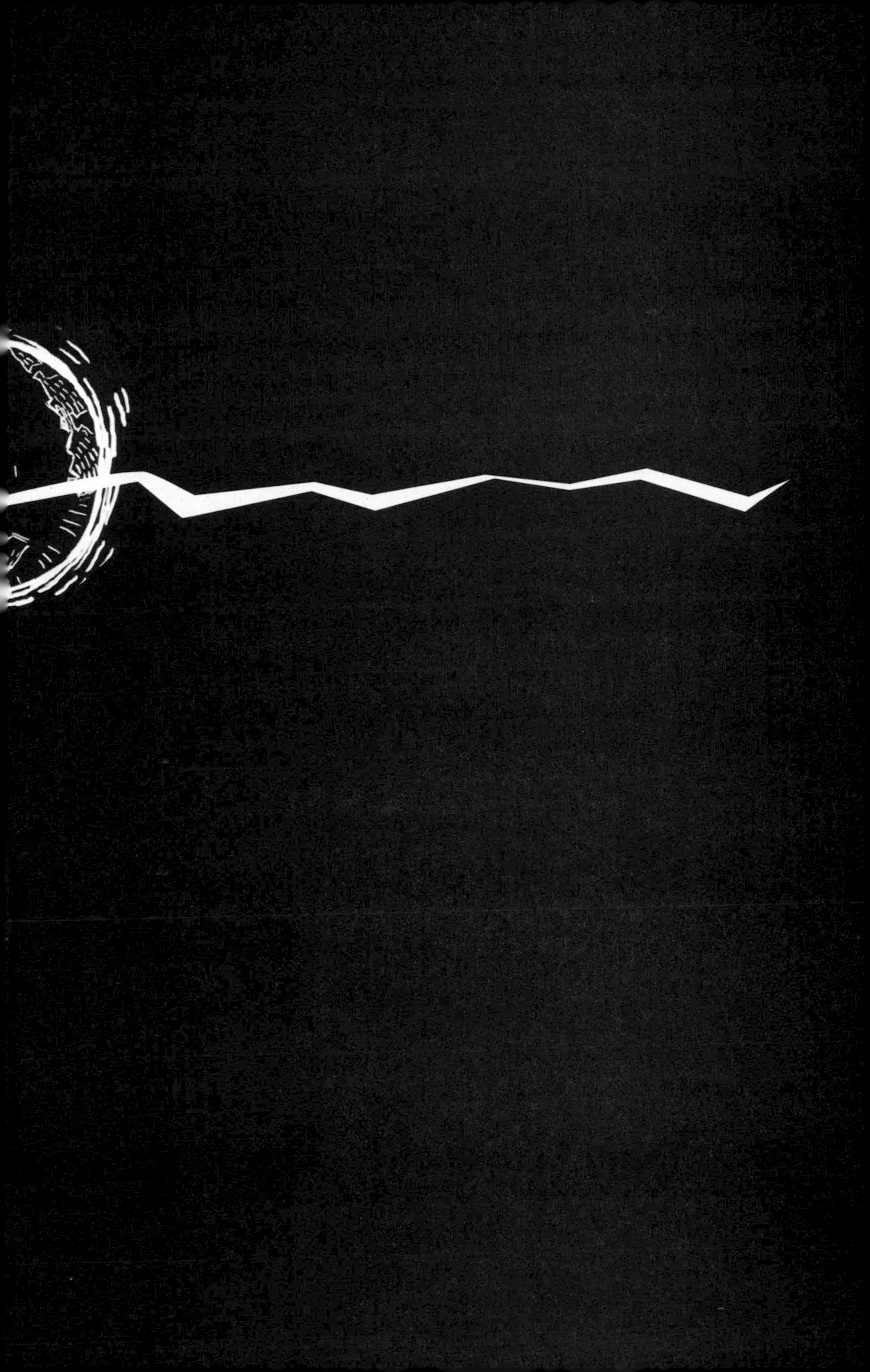

And that was good enough for him.